The Innocent Teacher

REKAWT A. BARZANJI

iUniverse, Inc.
New York   Bloomington

iUniverse books may be ordered through booksellers or by contacting:

iUniverse
1663 Liberty Drive
Bloomington, IN 47403
www.iuniverse.com
1-800-Authors (1-800-288-4677)

ISBN: 978-1-4401-8513-7 (sc)
ISBN: 978-1-4401-8514-4 (ebook)
ISBN: 978-1-4401-8515-1 (hc)

Printed in the United States of America

iUniverse rev. date: 10/27/2009

Dedicated to my mom and dad, angels of my life; my brothers and sisters; and my friends, who encouraged me in the writing of this book.

"What's remain at the end, it's the truth"

Contents

Acknowledgments

I am very grateful to my family and to Mallory Alicia, who always supported me and encouraged me during the writing of this book. I am grateful for her advice and information about editing and publishing and for reading some parts of my unfinished manuscript, which encouraged me to continue. I also am grateful to Kristine Gorney for her encouragement and support; and for my friends in my country: Omed Karadagy, who always supported me to write from the time I was seventeen; for Ary Barzanji, my best friend, and for his support; and for Aso Penjweny, Zanko, Bakhtear, and whoever supported me during this process.

In the Village

The dust emerged over the hilltop right after the gunshot was heard, but the little tomato-paste can that was used as a target was unmoved, its bright color sparkling in the sun.

"You still didn't get it," said Kak Rahman. "The bullet whizzed over it. Try one more time." Kak Rahman was a man I knew from my village. When my father was alive, he and Kak Rahman had been best friends.

"I wasn't holding tight enough. My finger slipped off the trigger," I explained.

"If there was someone there, you would have killed him by now. Never shoot a gun without holding it properly. You have to be careful," said Kak Rahman.

"How am I going to shoot it if I see someone standing there?" I asked.

"You going to hurt yourself. It will hurt your shoulder if you don't hold the gun tightly. You will learn gradually; you just need more practice. I want you to become the best and become a tough man," Kak Rahman explained, taking the rifle from me. "If you practice more, you will learn faster, and after that, we can go out more often." He remained silent for a few minutes, holding the gun, and then he added, "Especially when the hunting season comes. We can go out every evening to hunt rabbit. The valley has a lot of rabbits, so we can get some every day."

My name is Rebeen, and I am eighteen years old. I have light brown hair and a goatee beard, fair-skin, and a little scratch over my right eye, which was caused by a bullet shell when I was playing with my friends when I was ten. My friends opened fire and filled it with bullet shell. I was close to the fire, unaware of their actions. The bullet shell tip exploded, and hit me above my right eye. I was lucky that I didn't lose my eye.

"Were you born here in the village?" Kak Rahman asked me.

"No, I wasn't, but my father was," I replied.

Kak Rahman nodded. "Your father and I were born here in the village, and we also grew up here. We were best friends, though he was one year older than I. I still remember every square foot of this land we spent years together in the countryside; we were sons of the mountains." He checked the safety button on the rifle. "But his bad luck didn't let him live; his life was sacrificed for our liberty and this nation. His dream was to see this country's freedom and to see our flag flying at the top of the mountains and buildings all over the country. He was wounded few times, but it was not until the last time, during the summer of 1988, when helicopters bombarded the villages, that he died."

I listening to him, waiting to see if he'd let me try to shoot the target one more time.

"They said he was shooting the helicopter from under the tree when the 'copter fired at him," Kak Rahman explained. "He died right there. At that time he was on duty around the Karadag area for a month, but they sent me to the Sharbazer area; I wasn't with him." Kak Rahman checked his pocket for no apparent reason. "The last I knew of your father, he'd given a letter to one of our friends, who went back to the city for a short time and gave the letter to your mom. After that,

I never saw him again. I heard about a month later that he had been killed."

I was impatiently waited for Kak Rahman to finish "Can I try one more time? I will do better this time" I asked him again as he sat on the big rock and folded his hands over his chest.

Kak Rahman handed me the rifle as he continued, "In reality, my friends hid the news from me because they knew that your father and I were like brothers, and the time wasn't right to give me the news that he had died—we were in the war, and I was in charge of a group at that time." He released a big sigh. "I am really sorry for you and your family." I said nothing, and we both kept quiet for a few minutes; then he asked, "Do you remember when your father died? I believe you were seven or eight years old at that time."

"Yes, I do remember. My mom still keeps the letter, and when his friends brought back my father's corpse, my relatives kept it a secret so that the government would not take all of us to prison. We buried my father secretly and we didn't hold a funeral for him either. I believe they washed his body in a friend's house and put him in a coffin. Our relatives and friends came in little groups at a time, one after another, but no one knew it was a funeral. I remember my mom sobbing for months and always looking at his picture, holding it in her hands against her breast for hours. She kissed the picture and cried every day." I sat on the little rock opposite to where Kak Rahman setting "Most of the time my mom makes me cry too. For almost ten years after my father died, my mother never changed her dark funeral clothes. Then, one day, my uncle came to the house and talked to her. He also gave her some money to buy herself new clothes. He told her to get rid of the black clothes she had worn for the past ten years. Why do folks wear black clothes to grieve the loss of loved ones?" I inquired. "It doesn't change any essential fact or bring back the one who left the living world. In reality, the other world is the real, living world, not here."

"As a matter of fact, it doesn't bring back the dead to the living world," Kak Rahman agreed. "But it's became a custom for people, when they lose their loved ones, to wear black for a long time. As you know, our country went through a lot of opposition because we're Kurdish people, divided between four countries for almost a hundred years now."

"Where you were born?" I asked Kak Rahman.

"I was born here, like your father," he replied. "We were friends until the day he left us all. I really miss him; he was one of the best men I have ever known in my life. I know you miss him, too, but because you were a little when he passed away, you don't know what type of man he was." Kak Rahman lit a cigarette and puffed the smoke out—he'd been smoking since he was sixteen. "If I didn't see him for a single day, I thought the day had passed by with out any interesting things happening, or I'd think I missed some thing important. He was a symbol of friendship and unity; I never ever tired of him," he explained.

"My mom always talked about his companion and compassion—what a friendly character he was. He once told my mom that he hoped I would follow in his footsteps. He even wrote this in his letters," I said. "He mentioned it in that letter you talked about earlier, and because of that, I want to be a son of the mountain, too. I want you teach me how to shoot. I want to be a good shooter of our foe, to shoot those who killed my father."

Kak Rahman nodded silently while enjoying his cigarette. Finally, he said, "I understand your feeling, but I want you keep in mind that the day your father was killed, we were at war with the enemy. We fought against them in our towns and cities, and we have secret members in all cities—they're very active." He pointed his index finger toward me, as if to stress his lesson. "The only place that was left for us was these great mountains, but the horrible government still doesn't want us to be in our mountains. They wanted to kick us all away from the border, and at the same time they captured our old parents or siblings or anyone they could get." He dropped the cigarette butt on the dirt and stepped on it. "They forced the entire family to prison and tortured them however they wished. They raped our women in their prisons. Some of them were still alive when they came out during the revolution of 1991,those who were found before they were killed—because when the revolution started, we kicked out all the government organizations in our cities. I think you remember that."

"No, I don't. I was five years old," I replied. Then I gave it some thought. "Well, yes, I do remember my mom talking about it sometimes," I corrected myself.

"Some females, when they were captured, were virgins," Kak Rahman informed me. "But all of them had one or two babies when we freed them during the revolution days. You know what I mean?" asked Kak Rahman.

"Yeah, I know. I heard all of them, but you know what?" I shrugged. "Seems like we've already forgotten all this. Nowadays, who care how much sacrifice you or your father did in the past? Every high-ranking official forgot about those who shed their blood for this day to come." I was frustrated. "Each of them has a high type of living. I heard some of them say that they built a great house with the best design, and they even have a swimming pool in their house. Not only that, they've also slept with a different woman each night, and whenever they want, they get a new wife. Almost every four or five years, they change wives like they change cars, as soon as the new model arrives. Some of them, of course, have more than one wife. They practice religion for that purpose, but they never pray five times a day. They drink, and they are still not satisfied with their wives. They look for whores to sleep with or whenever they see a sixteen- or eighteen-year—old, they get married to them without thinking about the big difference in age between them. They forgot when they were in the mountains, and they don't even have a donkey to ride sometimes."

"Well, not all of them are alike anyway," he said, trying to cool me down. "Maybe what they say is a little too much, but I am sure the one who told you all that is just angry with them." He scratched the back of his neck with his right hand, trying to find right words. "Whatever. We still have to follow the way that men like your father opened up for us to survive this country. Don't listen to such folks who make you despair of continuing the liberty of this wonderful homeland of ours. I believe we should keep our unity and not give up our hopes." He tried to change the subject. "Did you guys have a plan to go back to the city this winter, or are you staying here?"

"Well, I guess I am staying, but I don't know about my mom and her husband. I believe if they stay, then my sisters and little brothers also will stay, but they don't mention such matters," I said frankly. "I will stay until the end of September, but I don't really want to stay over for winter. You know when it snows, it's hard. I don't really like it."

"I believe you should remain here and help your mom, not leave her alone," Kak Rahman advised me. "Did you really like her husband, Kak Jalal, or not? Seems that you kind of have some trouble with him, don't you?"

"No, I like him," I replied with a smile. "He's a poor man, but he never said anything bad to me. Besides, my mom is happy with him. There is not any trouble between us , but as you know, I am a city boy. There's nothing wrong with being a village boy or girl, but I spent most of my time in the city, and I grew up in the city."

"If that's the way you like it, it's up to you," said Kak Rahman. "Oh, are you going to school?"

"Not really. I quit school long ago," I informed him. "I wasn't really enjoying it. It's too much for me, with the type of life I lead."

"Why is that? You're smart enough to finish your schooling and get a degree." He seemed disappointed. "Maybe you can become a teacher and come back here to serve your village. Teachers get good benefits, not good enough, I know, but it's better for your future when you retire," he explained, I kept silent, than he added "It's not a good idea to quit."

"It's too late for that suggestion," I replied. "Nowadays, the teachers are poor and leading a very poor life." I gave a sigh. "As I told you, I quit school a long time ago."

"But you always can go back and continue," Kak Rahman explained.

"I don't have a desire to go back to school anymore," I said clearly.

"What do you mean, you don't have a desire for school?" Kak Rahman inquired.

"I don't know. I just don't like school. Do you know what those people who finished school do now? Let me tell you. I have a friend whose brother finished engineering tech, but right now, he's pushing a cart in the middle of the city market, moving the loads of goods from the city alleys. His education doesn't benefit for him or suit his needs. There are a lot of examples like," I explained

"But he's not staying like that forever. Some day, things will change, and he will find a place that's hiring in his field," he advised me. "This work he does now is just temporary. Nothing's in its place nowadays, but things get change, sooner or later, so you better listing to my advice. When you go back to the city, go back to school. How long have you been away from school anyway?" he inquired

"It's quite a while, almost four years now," I said. "But I want to go back to the city to find a job. Living there, maybe I will come back for next summer, but I don't know yet."

"So who will you live with while the rest of your family is here?" asked Kak Rahman.

"We still have a house in the city. Besides, I have my uncle's house and my aunt's," I replied.

"Whatever you do, enjoy it, but we'll miss you," Kak Rahman replied gently.

"Thank you. I will miss you, too. I really enjoy spending time with you on nice evenings like this," I told him.

"I guess it's getting late. Seems like we've had not much luck with hunting anything today, but we will try tomorrow," he said. "Let us find some wood to take home at least. We better not head back empty-handed."

We began to collect bamboo around in the forest, and then I asked, "Don't you go back to the city in the near future?"

"Maybe next month, I think," replied Kak Rahman.

"Be my guest whenever you arrive," I said.

"Sure enough," he replied. "I would like to."

The sun's beams gently fell from the west, like an orange hiding behind its leaves. The shade of the high mountains replaced the light of the day as we made our way back to the village. The rifle hung from Kak Rahman's shoulder, and we carried bamboo in our hands as I followed him, making our way back home on the dusty, narrow road.

Three Months Earlier in Sunshine High School

The bell rang in the school, while pupils at the Sunshine High School for Girls in the Ashty district roamed around the schoolyard. Some of them were busy with their assignments, while others were busy talking about different aspects of their lives. They all were young and had their own dreams and daily life problems. A bunch of girls were walking, with their books open in their hands, studying for upcoming examinations. Some were telling jokes and laughing out loud. A girl, walking arm in arm with two of her friends, stopped walking to use her cell phone. Her name was Zeno, and she had a slim figure, with long hair that fell down from her shoulders and black eyes shaped like almonds. She also had nice lips—over her upper lip was a black dot mark, and she wore a nose stud piercing in the right side of her nostril. She wore a short black skirt to her knees with a white polyester shirt, and a pair of white cotton knee socks. After she finished checking her text messages, she thrust the cell phone back in her book bag, and then the girls headed to their class.

They sat in their chairs, waiting for the teacher to arrive. When the English teacher showed up, all the students rose in respect.

"Good morning, girls," said the teacher, who had a copy of the English book in her hand, along with a copybook for recording students' scores. She was about forty years of age.

"Good morning," the students chanted in response.

"Today we will start with the dialogue from the last time we read," said the teacher. "Everyone should have it memorized by now, as I instructed you last time." She walked through three rows of chairs and stood at the back of the room, facing the blackboard. "You, Galawez," she said, pointing to one of the students. "You are Mrs. Brown." She pointed to another student. "Jwan, you are Mr. Brown—sorry that there are no males here so that you have to become Mr. Brown." The students start chuckling. They finished the dialogue perfectly and sat back in their places. The teacher went on with other students and marked their grades in her copybook.

After the class was over, they had a ten-minute break. Some students went to the school cafeteria; others went to the schoolyard. Zeno, the girl who was walking in the schoolyard earlier with her friends, Sarah and Shler, went to a corner at the far side of the school building. Zeno took the cell phone from her pocket and dialed her mother's number.

"Hi, Mom, it's me," said Zeno"How are you?" Zeno waiting for her mom to respond

"I don't know yet," Zeno said, "But I can take Sarah and Shler like before, if M want me"

"I'm not able to come this time," Shler said.

"Why can't you?" Sarah asked. "I will come," she assured Zeno.

"Sarah will come with me, but Shler said she can't," Zeno informed her mom. Suddenly, she grimaced a little bit. "I can't find anyone else." Zeno told her mother. "I asked three of my friends last week, and they almost punched me in the face when I told them." She paced as she spoke to her mother. "Now, they don't even talk to me."

"I told you that I will come," Sarah reassured her.

Zeno looked at Sarah with a smile. "Mom says he's asking for fresh one," Zeno informed her friends.

"That's Sarah," Zeno replied to her mom.

"Mom said he's like you so much," Zeno informed Sarah

.

"Anyway, I'll try to find one, but I don't know for sure." Zeno finally said

"Good-bye now. I'm going to be late for class," Zeno finally said and cut the connection. By this time, the schoolyard was almost empty, and as the bell rang, they ran back to the class.

One of the students was erasing the blackboard when Zeno, Sarah, and Shler entered the classroom. The student was a class inspector who had a list of students' names in the class and was in charge of reporting absent individuals. All the students took their seats as they waited for the teacher to arrive. They waited for some time but the teacher didn't show up, so the class inspector announced that she would go to the school office to ask about the teacher. She left, and the students roamed around the room, talking to each other.

"I bought new jeans with a red sweater last week," Zeno informed her friends.

"Yeah, why you don't wear it?" Sarah asked.

"I wore it last Friday, when we went to visit the government official M with my mom," said Zeno.

"Oh, you guys went to his house on Friday?" Shler inquired.

"Yeah, almost every Friday we pay him a visit," Zeno explained.

"You mean with your mom?" Shler asked, impressed.

"Yeah, with my mom," replied Zeno.

"Do you guys do anything?" Sarah asked.

"Of course. If not, why we would go there?" Zeno said.

"For how long?" Shler asked.

"About two to three hours," Zeno said, smiling.

"Did he do it with you, too, or just your mom?" Sarah inquired.

"Both of us," replied Zeno, "but he said to my mom that he wants to be with me more. He said he wants to educate me, and he sure did."

"So what's your mom say?" Shler asked, impressed.

"She said it's okay as long as it's not hurting me," Zeno informed them.

"Why? Did he hurt you before?" Sarah interrupted.

"Yeah, when he got so horny, he smacked me on my butt," Zeno explained with a smile. "But it's nice, though."

"What did he say in response?" they both asked.

"He told my mom it's okay and that she shouldn't worry about it," Zeno explained.

"Is Nazdar really your mom?" Shler asked with a serious look on her face.

"Yes, she is," Zeno lied. "Why are you asking me this?"

"I don't know," replied Shler.

"What about your dad?" Sarah interrupted.

"He died long ago," Zeno replied.

"So why do you live with your sister instead of your mom?" they both asked her.

"The truth is that she's not my mom," Zeno said. "Are you happy now?"

"Then who is she?" they asked.

"She's just a old neighbor of ours. My sister also knows her," Zeno explained, "but my sister doesn't know about what we do. One day I went shopping with her; then she said she wanted to visit a friend. She took me there, and we went in. When I saw the man I recognized him right away. I saw him many times on TV. Then, after some talk, right in front of me Nazdar took off her clothes and started having fun. They both deceived me. I am young. I got horny, and we did it," Zeno explained.

"Wow," Shler and Sarah said in response.

"Nazdar told me, to invited you to M's house he will be surprised, after M was satisfied with me, then she said if anyone asked when we're together who I am? say that I'm your mom, until no one notice why we're going out so often, and that way when you invited your friends, they don't think that what we are about to do it's danger" One of the student, who was a class inspector, got back from office and informed all students in the class, that their teacher will not come today, they should wait until time for next class, then Zeno and her friends walked out to the schoolyard to meet with other students.

"I want to ask Deren to M's house for today," said Zeno. "What do you think of my pick?"

"She's not bad," said Sarah, "but I don't know if she can come."

"We can try and see what she says," Shler interrupted. She was eager to find someone to cover for her.

"Yep, I just give her a shot," said Zeno, then she release a sigh. "See what she says."

The girls walked toward Deren as she sat on a bench, talking to her friends and playing a game on her cell phone.

"How you guys doing?" asked Zeno.

"Fine, how are you doing?" answered Deren and her friends.

"Not much, just wandering around," Zeno replied. "Deren, did you pass the math examination last month?"

"No, I didn't. The math teacher doesn't like me, I guess," said Deren. "She always picks on me in class."

"Well, if you don't want to be bothered," said Zeno, "just study a little more and she will leave you alone."

"Whatever," Deren said. "I don't much like math anyway."

"Suit yourself," Zeno said.

Deren stood, and she started to walk away, but Zeno linked her arm through Deren's arm. They walked around for a while.

"If I ask you a favor, do you promise me not to tell anyone what I asked you?" Zeno asked with a sigh. "What I am going to tell you must stay between us, okay?"

"I promise," replied Deren after she gave it some thought.

"First, I want to ask you a question," Zeno said. "Do you have a boyfriend?"

"Why do you ask me that question?" Deren said.

"I just want to know," replied Zeno, "if you don't mind, of course."

"Not really," Deren said frankly.

"Not even one?" Zeno inquired.

"Not even one," Deren assured her, "but there are some guys that are always wandering around me on my way to school."

"Do any of them ever ask you out?" Zeno inquired.

"Two of them did," Deren said, "but they didn't ask with words."

"Do you have any feeling for them? Do you like any of them?"

"Not really," Deren replied. "I ignore them."

"Okay, then," said Zeno. "If I ask you something else, will you reply honestly, just like the first question?"

"Yes, I will. What is it that you want to ask?"

"I don't know how to put it," Zeno begin, "but do you promise you're not going to tell anyone?"

"No, I won't," Deren assured her.

"Let me tell you what I have. You're not the only one I asked," said Zeno. "Before now, I asked Sarah and Shler, and they agreed with me. I don't push them. To be frank with you, they chose to do what I asked."

"What is it, then?" Deren inquired.

"There is a guy I'd rather not tell you his name for now."

"Okay," said Deren.

Zeno tilted her head and thought for a moment. "There's a man; he's a government official. He's rich, of course, and we go to his house once a week, on Thursdays," said Zeno, "because that's a day when he has time. I also go on Friday, so we go after school for a few hours, and we have fun with him. You know what I mean when I say fun?"

"Yeah, I guess I know what you mean," replied Deren. "Having sex, right?"

"Precisely," said Zeno. "You are a smart girl; I knew it."

"When are you going there?" Deren inquired. "Today is Thursday; you said Thursday, right?"

"Yes, we're going after school," Zeno informed her.

"Okay, I will," Deren agreed. "To tell you the truth, I've had sex a few times."

"Wow, you said you don't have a boyfriend."

"I do, but just in the behind, as they say" Deren said, grinning.

"At least you have experience."

"It happened few months ago," Deren informed her.

"Where? And with whom?" Zeno inquired.

"A guy I met at the book fair," replied Deren.

"You're not going to tell me?" inquired Zeno.

"It's totally confidential," said Deren. "Please don't push me."

"Anyway, that's fine with me. So you will come or not?" Zeno asked.

"I guess I will," Deren replied, "but shouldn't you tell me who he is first?"

"You will know when you get there," replied Zeno. "I promise."

"I want to know now," said Deren. "What if he happens to be someone I'm related to?"

"Oh, don't worry," Zeno assured her. "I'm sure you're not related to him."

"Okay, then where are you going to take me?" Deren inquired. "I mean, in the house, car, or where?"

"A car!?" said Zeno surprisinly "He have a big house. Why in the car?"

"I just ask" Deren said

"Why? The guy in the book fair took you to his car?"

"Most of the time, yes," replied Deren. "One time in a house, too."

"His house, you mean?" Zeno inquired.

"Kind of," said Deren, "but I'm not sure."

"Did anyone live there?" asked Zeno. "Or he was alone?"

"I don't know, but when I went, we were alone."

"What do you mean, you don't know?" Zeno inquired.

"Hell, why should I care?" she's grimaced. "At least he knows it's a safe place."

"Okay, take it easy," said Zeno.

After a short silence, Deren inquired, "Does he have a big one?"

"You mean his thing or the house?" Zeno didn't get it.

"His thing, not the house," Deren clarified.

"Hm, he has a giant one," Zeno said pleasingly.

"Wow," said Deren.

"Are you worried?" Zeno asked. "You can handle it."

"Not a problem," replied Deren. "Bigger is better."

"Okay, we'll see after school," said Zeno.

"Absolutely," Deren agreed.

Zeno and Deren wandered around the schoolyard until the bell rang. Ten minutes later. the science class started, when they done, they went to the official house along with Sarah, but Shler excused herself that day.

"Let him know I'm on my period," Shler said, making an excuse.

"But you are not?" asked Zeno.

"It's my excuse, okay?" said Shler.

"Okay, don't worry," t Sarah replied.

Shler walked home alone, but Sarah and Deren went along with Zeno. They took a taxi, and Zeno paid for the cab. Fifteen minutes later, they got to his house .

Another Day in the Village

The sound of a braying donkey in the village on a chilly morning woke me up. I opened my eyes, carefully scanning the room before moving my body from my shabby bed. I saw my mom, Gullzar Khan, sitting by the fireplace, eating breakfast. The kettle of hot water and a small teapot were placed over the top on the fire. In the other corner was an earthenware jar full of water, and beside the jar was an aluminum bowl. I slowly began moving my legs and felt that my pajamas were wet. I scanned the room carefully one more time; I knew what had happened to me right away. My Mother was still sitting by the fireplace, chanting a prayer. She was a very strong believer in her own faith. Then I closed my eyes, pretending not to be awake yet, but I listened for her movement. I wished she'd leave the room, and finally, after a little wait, she went out into the small hall.

When I was assured of her absence, I jumped out of bed and grabbed my baggy pants that were hanging on a nail on the wall. I put them on as fast as I could, then tried to gather my thoughts about the dream I'd had last night.

The dream was about a woman I used to see when she sat in front of her house. She was unaware that her long gown did not fully cover her legs as she was sat on the doorstep, enjoying the sunlight, and her underwear was visible as she swayed her legs. That was back in the city last autumn, about ten months ago. Why in the world would I dream about that mature woman last night? I thought I saw the same image of her in my dream that now caused my pajamas to be moist. I'd had a wet dream last night; there is no doubt about it.

Now I remembered who she was. I tried to forget about the dream to hide my hard penis and to calm down. I pushed it back in my pants, but for some reason it didn't work. I decides to go back under my blanket for a little longer before my mom returned to the room. I tried not think about sex at all for a while. Shortly afterward, my mom came back.

"Are you not awake yet my son?" asked my mom, Gullzar Khan.

I tried to ignore her, but as soon as I heard her call, I was back to normal mode. I moved the blanket over my head, yawning once, then rubbed my eyes a few times. Finally, I got out of bed. The clock hanging on the wall showed it was 6:30 AM.

"Did you sleep with your pants on last night?" my mother asked me. "Why were you cold?" She was holding a bowl of sour cream in her hand.

"Not all night; just a little while ago I put them on," I replied. "Anyway, I'm going to the fountain in the woods to wash my face. I will be back." Then I left the room.

"Okay, be careful out there. It's still dark. Come back soon," my mom hollered at me.

"Maybe I'll take a little shower if no one's around. I'll take a bucket with a towel; don't worry," I said from the corridor.

"Why take a shower now?" she ask me, but I ignored the question, and she went on, "Don't forget it's by the water tank. I will get your breakfast ready."

Gullzar Khan sipped her tea with a sugar cube in her moth, while sitting by the fireplace. I went out to the little alley and walked toward the fountain area. It was still dark but the sky was brightening. I increased my pace, wishing that no one would show up before I finished my shower. Most of the villagers did not come out from their homes at this time, except for the village shepherd who herds the sheep from south of the village.

As soon as I reached the fountain, I took off my clothes and hung them on the small branch of a tree. I took a quick shower and dried myself with a towel. My teeth chattered in the chilly morning air, and I tried to dry my hair as best as I could with a towel. Then I went back home.

I sat down by the fireplace to get warmed up and started eating my breakfast. My mother put a hot glass of tea with a Sour Cream and butter in front of me, along with fresh homemade bread.

"Your uncle went to the woods, and he took a donkey with him to bring back some wood," my mother informed me. "He already carried the axes and the saw, He told me he wants you to help him, but be careful, my son, not to injure yourself. I'll have lunch ready when you come back at noon."

"How long ago did he leave?" I asked.

"Not very long ago, about a half-hour or so." She munched the sugar cube in her mouth. "Hopefully, today you'll be able to finish chopping the wood, because tomorrow you have to work on the farm. I will be helping you in the field. We better finish all the work before cold season approaching us, we will get tire during the winter, if we don't save enough supplies now" My mom explained

"Why me?" I inquired.

"What do you mean?" asked my mom.

"I am going back to the city before the weather getting cold," I said. "I wouldn't stand here with the snow falling in a small village like this. It's not easy to go anywhere when snow covers everything and the road shuts down for days. It's not worth it," I explained. "I don't know what kind of pleasure you have, living in a place like this. You should all come back to the city for winter."

When my mom heard that suggestion she said, "Are you serious or just joking around?"

"I am serious. Why would I joke?"

"Because we haven't seen snow for the last couple of years—that's not an excuse. And how will you live? Who will cook for you or wash your clothes? Where will you sleep?"

"In the hotel, I guess," I said sarcastically. "In our house, of course."

"But how can you manage to live in the big house like that alone?" my mom inquired.

"Do you think I'm scared? That is why you married that man, I guess. You're scared!" I said jokingly.

"Are you angry with your uncle?" She smiled. "He's just like your father. Is there anything wrong between you and him?

"No, nothing's wrong between us. He's a good man, and I'm not angry with him. I just don't want to live here. I want to go home." I chewed the bread and then said, "After all, I don't mind coming back here for a visit next summer. I enjoy hunting and working in the woods, even though it's not an easy task to chop wood and collect it, but when I go back to the city, I will find something to do. You don't have to worry about me," I explained.

"I am going to worry," she said, "because I'm a mother. I don't want you to work making money for me, but what are you going to do in the city? I mean, what kind of work do you have in mind? If it's about money, I can ask your uncle if he will give you money. What do you say, sweetie?"

"No, it's not about money. I just miss the city. I am tired of this place. I want a change of air." I tried to give her some reason.

"Change of air? Where is air fresher than on this mountainside?" she asked.

"That's not what I mean; not that kind of air. I'm a city boy, you know, and I don't want to stay here through all four seasons. I would like to go back to the city, and no one can stop me."

"You're a man, I know, thank the Lord, but honey, you're just eighteen. You still need someone to watch after you. I am your mom, and I want you stay with us. I carried you for nine months and nine days in my tummy. I spend many nights and days raising you. Is this how you reward my hard work?" she inquired.

I didn't know how to respond. "I am not leaving you forever, Mom. I am going back to the city to find a job. I will work there," I explained. "Also, my uncle's and my aunt's houses are available. I am sure they are fine with that, so why do you make such a big deal about it? As you say, I'm eighteen now. If it was during Saddam's times, if I quit school he would take me to the army by force. That's proof that I'm a man, and I already told you, I'm not staying here all year. Please stop worrying about me. Let me grow up. If I find a job, I can help you, too, so you should support me, not frighten me."

"I don't want you to help us. We're fine, honey. We'll help you with whatever you want," she offered. "You have no idea that I went through how much trouble until I raised you, letting your uncle finish his work and collecting the products on the farm. I'm sure he will buy you anything you want, but please don't leave us. Try to understand what I am telling you. He needs your help, because he cannot manage to do all this hard work alone, and I am sure he didn't expect you to leave him at this time of year, when he really needs your support." I kept quiet so she went on, "I'm sure you'll also deserve his support someday, and he will be there for you when you need him, so you better change your mind now. What do you say, sweetie? I'm begging you!"

"That's funny," I said. "On one hand you tell me you don't want my help, and on the other hand, you say he needs my help. What's that suppose to mean, Mom? I am not leaving you right now. I said that I am not staying over for winter. Before snow starts falling, I will leave, and snow will start within a few weeks. But now I will stay until all the work is done. Then I'm expecting some money from him. Besides, I'm not going back to the city for fun. I will look for a job. I'm not asking him for his money. I work, and as you say, I should get paid for what I do."

"I know, honey. He will pay you. Do you think he spends the money he makes on someone else? Of course not!"

"Yeah, he spends it on you and his children," I told her.

"What do you mean? You're also our child," she informed me.

"Only your child, not his," I explained.

"Don't be silly!" she said angrily. "I'm sure he loves you as much as he loves his own. My son, never say that in front of him."

"Why not? I'm your son, not his, and that's true. If I say that to him, why would he get mad at you?" I inquired.

"Maybe he'd think you dislike him. Do you really dislike him, honey?" my mom inquired.

"No, I told you—it's not about him; it's about me," I explained. "I guess I'm late. I'd better be going."

I put on a clean pair of socks and my shoes and then left the house at once, walking along the dusty alley of the village, greeting whomever I chanced to see on my way to the farm. Some little children emerged from their houses. Their faces were unwashed and some muck fell from their noses as they sat by the door, looking around at the passers-by. Flies buzzed around their heads, and sometimes they stuck out their tongues, licking the wet muck on their upper lips. The sparrows chirped in the tree branches and pigeons roamed in groups all around. Some people rode their cattle outside the village to the grassland close by. A man filled his donkey's back with chopped wood—he looked as tired as the donkey with a heavy burden on its back. He had a stick in his hand, and every once in a while, he slapped the donkey with it.

The women of the village walked toward the fountain located to the south. One of them had a plastic bucket on the top of her head. It was full of dirty clothes to wash. Most of them were children clothes. Another woman washed shit from her little kid's ass with water in a small bucket in front of their house. The little boy cried out because of the cold water. Then she put a new pair of pants on him after drying his body with a small towel. She kissed him on the cheek, and I started thinking about myself when I was that boy's age, but of course, I wasn't able to recall those memories.

After reaching the woods, I heard the sound of chopping wood. *Must be my uncle*, I thought. As I got closer I saw that he already had finished part of the work. Sweat was falling down from his face.

"Good morning, Uncle!" I shouted to greet him.

He stopped chopping wood and put the ax down, turning his face toward me. "Good morning, son. Finally, you're awake," Kak Jalal replied with a smile.

"Yes, I am. I guess it's your turn to take a rest, and I will finish it," I offered.

He sat on a big branch of wood and took out the handkerchief from his back pocket. Kak Jalal wiped the sweat from his forehead and face. "We better finish this cutting today," he suggested. "Tomorrow, I must try to do the farming work." He was exhausted and took a deep breath before he continued. "If we can make the producce ready this week and take them to the city market, we can relax until the second part of the products are grown, but I want you go to the farm later and water those tomatoes, eggplants, and zucchinis. Just remove the block on the water canal and let it run through the land. That's all you have to do for today. Be careful and watch out for snakes or scorpions. Those dangerous creatures come out in the summer season, so we have to be aware of them. I'm going to go check the farm for a while. Before I get back, you go to the water the farm, as I told you. I will take the wood back home, riding the donkey," he explained to me.

"Why don't you water the farm, if you're going there now, as you said?" I suggested.

"I am not going that far inside the farm. I'm just checking it from the fences to see what became of it," he replied.

"Okay, I will finish the wood, and you can take it home then," I said.

"Sounds good," Kak Jalal agreed.

He left me and headed toward the farm, which is located on the west side of the forest., I saw him peer over the farming land, blocking the sun from his eyes by holding up his left hand. He checked the farm closely, studying the products around the fence. Finally, he got in the field and took some zucchini, putting it in the plastic bag he had in his pocket. By the time he got back I had finished chopping the wood and had it loaded on the donkey's back to take it home. The bag of zucchini in hand, he took the donkey's leash and started heading back home, while I collecting myself, ready to go to the farm to water the plants.

"How are the products going?" I asked him.

"Not bad, and that's the way it's suppose to be after all this hard work we did," he said. "We should continue to take care of it."

"Are you going to collect it soon and take it to the city market?" I asked.

"Yeah, we will, but not today; in a few days. Why are you in such a hurry?" Kak Jalal stopped.

"I thought we would start collecting them today," I replied.

"If you just be patient we will done you see," he said, "But when I left here to the city do better than now in the farm.

Don't let anyone or anything, especially animals like cattle or sheep, go in the farm and destroy all the products."

"I thought you were going to let me take the products to the city market," I said worriedly.

"No, I'll take it myself," he informed me. "Have you ever sold products in the city market before?" Kak Jalal complained.

"No, I haven't," I replied frankly, "but I can try it."

"So that means you should stay and I will go," he demanded.

"Okay, when you are going to leave, though?" I ask anxiously .

"Whenever I am ready; maybe after tomorrow," he said frankly.

"It's okay with me, but what will you do when you come back?" I inquired.

"What do you mean? I guess I'll take a rest," he replied.

"I mean, will you need my help anymore?"

"Why? What did you have in mind?" Kak Jalal asked suspiciously.

"Frankly speaking," I begin, "I am tired here, so I would like to go back to the city." I gave him a hint of smile and continued. "You know, I grew up there. I deserve to be there. I mean, it's nice to live on the countryside but not all year round. Maybe you're used to it, but I'm not. Hopefully you won't mind what you've heard, but that's what I feel right now. I really miss all my friends. You know, all my friends are there." I waited for him to say something, but the man stayed calm. "I suggest you all come back to the city for the winter, because when snow starts, you won't be able to get out, and it will be like locking yourself in the jail. You won't be able to walk around when there is more than three feet—sometimes four feet—of snow covering the area. You see what I mean?"

"No, I don't get it," he said sarcastically.

"After all, it's up to you to decide, but I can't stay any longer. I'll probably go back before winter takes over." I moved my right hand, directing it at him. "Now, you may ask what I will do when I'm alone or how I will manage when I've never lived on my own, but I am a grown man now. I can trust in myself. After all, I should start thinking about the future; try to find out who I am and what should I do with my life, and it's not that simple." I searched for the right words to continue. "Things change around you every day. You should try to fit yourself to it, but try not to harm anyone else." I was kind of giving advice. "To be honest with you, I believe it's time to say thank you for those years that you helped me out. I always try to be a nice person to you. As you know, I didn't spend much time with my beloved father; he died before I could get to know him. You've always helped me a great deal. and I appreciate all your hard work and patience. I promise you to be a person of whom you can be proud in return for being respectful and honest with my mother. You are my stepfather but almost a father. I care for you as you do for me, but I have made my decision: I will go back to the city soon. I hope this isn't upsetting to you." I spoke my mind, and it was a release for me.

Kak Jalal sighed as he thought for a moment. He looked at me straight in the eyes, collecting his thoughts. "I wonder what's making you think that way about us, son?" he inquired. "Leaving us as like this, this kind of farewell—as if you're heading to the battlefield? You should listen to me if what you said is true." I said nothing. "You know what? I love you as much as I love my children. It's not safe for you to live in the big house all alone." He pushed for a moment; I froze in place without word. He went on, "Nowadays, there is a lot of danger—things going on out there on a daily basis, life changing, people changing. But my dear son, people change not for good but for evil. Every day we hear all those terrible stories, most of them with teenagers like yourself. I know you're a good boy, but I don't think it's a good idea to live on your own right now." He hesitated for a moment while I listened to the birds singing in the trees. "You are just eighteen. We can't allow you to go astray; that's our responsibility. It's one of the reasons we came back to our village, to keep you with your brothers and sister away from all the craziness going on out there on a daily basis . We were really afraid to leave you alone in the big city."

He waited for me to say something, but I remained silent so he went on, "On the other hand, the residents of the city are not the original residents. Right now, we can say that people from all around country and neighboring countries come to the city for different purposes. There are too many things going on, things that never existed in our city before, such as drug deals, prostitution, and terror. Now, groups of teenagers are caught by the police for using drugs. I don't want you to go back to the city, my dear son, but if you promise me to be a good boy and listen to your uncle, I will take you with me when I take the products to the city. I don't mean to hurt your feelings. Even if I do, it's better than your going through something horrible. I pray for God to protect you."

I remained silent for some time, digging into my thoughts, searching for the right words to respond. "No, you don't have to afraid about me doing evil acts" I manage to begin with "My point is looking for a job and start to depend on myself in life, also I can make your life easier that way, you can check on me anytime you want" I didn't want to give-up so easily "After all I still have my uncle there I am sure he's watching what I'm doing, so why you're worried?" I inquired

"How did you come up with this idea, anyway? Did your mom teach you or somebody else in the village?"

"My mom?" I said. "No way!"

"So who's not happy to see you standing by my side? I bet somebody is jealous to see my stepson standing by me. I love him and he loves me back, and I care for him. I bet they are trying to making you stray and told you not to listen to me because I am not your real father," Kak Jalal said. "Or maybe someone asked you what you are doing in the village, working on the farm, you're young, so go back to the city and enjoy your life. Is that it? A teenager most likely would believe someone's advice without thinking about what's good or bad." He took out a cigarette, lit it, and blew the smoke out from his nose. "Listen to me, son," he went on. "Anyone who teaches you to do anything besides me or your mom—don't buy it or think it's a perfect idea. No one else cares about your happiness. Listen to the advice your parents give. If you're not going to listen to me, I am can't push you, but keep that in mind if anything happen to you, I'm not responsible for that, okay?" He put his hat back on and released a big sigh. "After all, I never pushed you to do anything for me by force. I've treated you like my own son, and fathers never want to hurt their children. You can stay home if you like don't to come to the farm. I will manage on my own somehow. Before I married your mom, I lived in this place most of my life. I had all this farming land that I have now—my beloved father had only my help because my older brother went to the mountains to fight for the country, like your father did." He looked at my face with doubt, he read that in my eyes nothing can change my mind, but he went on "He also got wounded in the same battle as your father was killed. He was in bed for about a month or so, but eventually he died. I met your mother at his funeral. That's when I found that she was having a hard time with losing your dad. Until then, I hadn't thought about marriage. Our life wasn't easy like yours is now. We always were in the war with a dictator, and we had no time to think about getting married. Most of the time, we'd spend nights in this village, hidden from the special guards. The guards had what they called a security system, but in reality, they put too many innocent people in the prison. After torturing them without mercy, most of them died. Finally, my cousins pushed me to get married, and they recommended your mom for me. I already had seen her a few times, and she finally agreed to go out with me. This was a few years after she lost your dad, so that's how I came up with the idea of marriage."

Neither of us spoke for a few minutes. "How about your brother?" I asked, finally breaking the silence.

"What about him?" Kak Jalal didn't get it.

"He wasn't married?" I inquired.

"No, he was not," he replied. He grabbed a rope to tie the wood in a bundle before placing it on the donkey's back.

"Well, nobody in the village taught me or told me to go back to the city," I reassured him. "Neither did my mom. It was my own decision, but I must be honest with you: last week I received a letter from one of my best friends in the city. He told me all about what he's doing."

"Best friend?" he said mockingly

I didn't reply but continued what I'd started while he was loading the donkey, by the time Kak Rahman arrived but he didn't interrput "He found a job—a guard with some government official. He makes a good salary, and he can take a time off whenever he wants. He said in the letter that this job is not very hard; he just has to be careful. He also mentioned that one of his friends, who was a guard with him, quit the job. When I read this, I thought maybe it would be a good chance for me to get hired in his place." I hoped I was making my point clear to him. "Because I am sure they'll hire someone else to replacing him. My friend didn't intentionally tell me about this job opportunity; he doesn't know I'm ready to go back to the city. I don't have it in mind to apply for that job unless I don't get any other job—that'll be my last shot. And I didn't tell my mom about this because I know she'll disagree with me no matter what. I am sure she doesn't want to see me with a rifle hanging off my shoulder. She's so scared, she thinks if I became a guard today, by tomorrow I would be killed. I can't blame her after what happened to my dad."

"I don't blame your mom, either," Kak Jalal shot back. "Why should you think to put your life in danger at such a age? Weapons not a good friend, especially in that type of job," he said, facing Kak Rahman, who was still working on bundling wood.

"He mentioned to me that he wanted to go back to the city," Kak Rahman said, breaking the silence. "And I told him to stay here and help his mother."

"Like I say, being a guard is my last choice, not the first one," I explained. "Besides, my friend was just informing me what he is doing."

"And just to make myself clear, I didn't advise him to go to the city—just to let you know," said Kak Rahman innocently.

"No, I didn't mean you by saying that," Kak Jalal assured him. "If I didn't know what kind of man you are, I wouldn't walk with you." He tilted his head toward me, while I pointed the rifle to the tree, just for fun. "Why don't you think about some other job?" Kak Jalal suggested. "Do you live for your friend or for yourself? I don't know what to tell you other than to discuss this with your mom. She should know what's in that head of yours. I won't tell you to leave or not to leave. I am not saying anything." He turned toward Kak Rahman. "You're my witness!" Then he looked back at me. "But she's your mother and if you love her, you will listen to what she says and respect her. It that clear?" he demanded.

"Okay, you don't have to give further explanation. I understand your feelings, and I don't blame you, either, but this is my life. I will decide what to do with it, not someone else."

"No, you're so wrong, son." Kak Jalal starting to get angry because I was behaving childishly. "The one who is supposed to tell you what to do is your mom. I don't give a damn about helping you if you don't listen to her."

"Cool down, cool down." I tried to move the discussion in a better direction. "I don't want to run away from you. All I ask is to find a way to live on my own. I am not disobedient to you, I promise, but I am not a little kid anymore, so don't treat me like one. I have to find my way in life," I explained.

"What did you mean, find your way in life?" Kak Jalal inquired. "And what way are you going to find? You are scared of your own shadow; you're just a kid, son. What else do you expect to do? You refused to finish your school and gave it up for no reason. Nowadays, no one gets a job without education. What are you going to do in the city? What kind of guard will you make when you've never fired a bullet in your life? Let's say that position is already taken by someone else, what's your plan after that? You'll have no choice but to come back here once again, so why spend that money for nothing? And you also want us to go back to the city with you? Why? Let me tell you why: because you can't manage to live on your own."

"I will not come back," I assured him. "Regardless of whether I get this job, I grew up in the city, so I deserve to live there. That's the end of it."

Kak Jalal continued to complain. "You seem like you're on fire since the day you got here. I already knew that a city boy like you, who grew up on the asphalt roads, would not lead a life in the mountains, chopping wood, or doing the farming work, or being a shepherd. All you know is how to iron your clothes and oil your hair so you can stand in front of the girls' school without hardly any money in your pockets. I don't know what silly girl you will find who will follow you for your clean clothes, or your hairstyle, or your shiny shoes. Your grandfather—may our Lord grant him peace—was born in this village and lived and died here. He never saw a doctor, and he always was healthy—he never went to the city. Everyone during his time loved him, and he was a very generous person—maybe that's the reason he wasn't so wealthy. If anyone knocked on his door to ask for anything, he'd give it away. He was a king of his time, with good character; everyone loved and respected him. Most times, people in the village would come to him when they needed advice about anything."

Kak Rahman didn't want to get involved, so he said nothing.

Kak Jalal continued, "He was a wise person and had a lot experience in his life. He went through a lot difficulty, and because of that, people respected your father, too. Because your father sacrificed his life for this country, that made him more loved for what he gave to his country and his people. Now, they also love you, so you better not go astray or have any missteps. This is a reminder for you to know who your forefathers were and whose family you belong to. I am glad that you want to serve our country, but I don't recommend that you be a guard. You can serve better if you finish school, become a doctor or a teacher, and serve your country in those fields."

I hesitated for a moment to show I'd heard his words. Then I said, "I believe you know better than I do. Nowadays, most people want be police officers. You know that, don't you?"

"What do you mean? Is that what you have in mind?" Kak Jalal inquired.

"No, I don't, but now we also have a policewoman; did you know that?" I replied.

"Yeah, I heard that we have a policewoman now. The other day, that guy who brought the letter for you—the driver of the white Toyota truck; I can't recall his name."

"Kak Ali?" I reminding him.

"Yeah, that's him So I asked him why folks are interested in becoming a police officer nowadays? He said it's all about money" said Kak Jalal

"Yeah, that's true; they're paid a good salary," I informed him. "Also, most of them work two weeks a month. Some of them don't even show up except on payday. Crazy country with a funny government—and those people are still making more money than a teacher. Why bother going to school to became a teacher when I can make more money as a policeman?"

"Paying police more than a teacher?" said Kak Jalal. "Why should anyone think about teaching school? That's a trick to get youth to leave the school and face danger under the name of security and national safety. That's all a bunch of lies, this government we have now more worse than the former regime I don't know why people keep shutting their mouths from all those tyrants. We had a revolution to survive from the dictator and his regime, but as we've seen, this government worse than him. They're just trying to get their pockets full of money and deposit it in their bank accounts in Europe," Kak Jalal went on. "No one remembers God. No one thinks that some day, we will all die and forgotten like previous nations. Teenagers need schools, education, and science to serve this country, but as we've seen, they're all running away from this country, whenever they get a chance. They didn't see their future as being as bright as the future of those tyrants' sons and their families.

That's what bothering me and bother most people of the country, who's in high ranks they have what they want, and they forgot about people.

We kept listening to him, and he went on relentlessly. I was surprised he didn't run out of words.

"Our city, day after day, turns to worse. Now all our problems become women's freedom or teenagers' rights. As a matter of fact, our women always have been free, but when they talk about the freedom of women, it's that women don't want to listen to men at all. They want to act like women do in places like Europe, for example. If they see a man on the street, they take him home without listening to or respecting their parents. And they do whatever they like to do, which is not compare with our culture. After all, do they really let their wife and daughters behave like that? Of course not, so why should we let them drive our kids crazy. Besides, people do not have electric power or water in their houses—not even enough kerosene to heat their homes in the winter or to light the lamps. What do people do if they don't have any utilities in the house? How do they warm their homes? The government has not allowed us to chop wood. What good is the beauty of nature if I die from cold? Anyway we almost late, so we'd better hurry and finish what's left for today. We will discuss this matter with your mom when we get home."

We wiped the sweat and wood dust from our faces with handkerchiefs and drank the remaining water that was left in a plastic bucket we'd brought along. Then we headed back home through the dense shadow of trees and chirping birds as cool air blew through the leaves in the forest.

The Next Morning in the Village

In the morning, roosters started crowing outside, close by the house. I'd just opened my eyes when the sound reached my ears. Of course, it was one of the rooster we have at home. It was standing on the outside wall, puffing its feathers while crowing loudly. The black darkness of the night turned to gray. A person with good pair of eyes could recognize everything in the dim light. The world was breathing fresh morning air, beginning the new day. There always was a lot of work to do in the village—people never ran out of work, especially if they are in a farmer's family, spending most of their time in the meadow or in the forest, chopping trees for winter.

"Nowadays, in this particular place, things get worse day after day," Hewa had written in his letter that I received yesterday.

Hewa is my bestfriend about same age I am, one day when I was about ten, it happened that I went to their alley when a group of kids my age tried to fighting me, Hewa came and stopped them, he also claimed that he knows me, but the matter of fact it was a first time I saw him, than we became best friends "I'm not saying that there's no other place in the world worse than our country, but our country is one of the most unsafe countries on the planet. The price of everything is going up on a daily basis. The government we dream about for years, came out to be nothing, except a group of mafia, after all those years of sacrifices. . it seems like things are worse that they were. The result came out totally opposite. Anyone who opens his mouth has something to blame the government for. The electric power gets worse, year after year. They always complain that the reason is that we don't have enough rain during the year. They're right, though, on one hand, and the gas and kerosene prices keep going up. Even in the middle of the summer, people can't afford to buy oil, even when we have most of the oil fields around the globe. Everyone loses patience from all the untrue promises they hear on a daily basis. And the country is running out of security. Now and then, you'll hear something strange happened. Every other day in the newspapers, you'll see something horrible. No one care for others like before, and everyone tries to get rich and feed only themselves, no matter how. This doesn't only apply to ordinary people like me, I go with flow, but to those in charge of the country, like high-ranking folks—they're worse. The price of food has gone up in a way I've never seen before. Household robberies take place in the middle of the day they take gas bottles or break into the house when they found out no one is at home." Hewa wrote that he was now working as a guard with one of the government officials himself.

But here in the village, at least you know everyone around you, I thought. *It's safer than a busy city full of strange stories and strange people.*

Hewa wrote at the end of his letter: "One of the guards, who's a best friend of mine, quit and went to Europe last week. They're looking for someone to take his place right now." Hewa asked me to take this opportunity.

I looked around the room; the sunlight had not yet covered the village, and the air was still chilly. I put the blanket over my head and decided to stay in bed for another half hour or so. I thought about the unpleasant news that my friend Hewa had written in his letter. Of course, I never explained that part to my mom or anyone. I knew if I told them the whole truth, they might stop me from going back to the city.

I needed to urinate so I got out of bed, planning to go to the forest, which was just across from my house . The forest had several nice fountains, and the village had a nice view of forest at the east side. At the bottom of the mountains, fresh air always blew through the tall pine trees. When I was sure that I was only one in the room, I leaped out of bed and put on my pants and shoes. I went out from the house, and when I reached the forest, everything nice and calm. I took off my pants, sat by the bushes, and emptied my bladder. When I was finished cleaning myself with few pebbles, I put my pants on and covered my dirt with leaves, like some animals do. Then I put a circle of rocks around it so no one would step on the spot by mistake. I headed to the spring water to clean my nostrils of muck to wash my hands and face with soap I brought from home. The cool air blowing on my face made me fully awake. Then I headed back home, looking around the area but seeing nothing unusual. Everything was in its proper place, birds were chirping in the trees; I saw my mom come back from washing the dirty clothes in the other fountain, one arranged for women only. She carried the clothes in a plastic bucket on the top of her head.

"Good morning, are you awake, son?" said my mom.

"Good morning, Mom. Yes, I am awake. I'm not sleepwalking," I replied with a humorous tone.

My little sister Jwan ran to me with a smiling face, as if she hadn't seen me for so long. When she reached me, I embraced her to my chest, kissing her cheeks. "Good morning, my little sister," I said.

"Good morning, my little brother," she teased.

I smiled at her. "No, I'm not a little brother; I'm older than you. You're a sweet little sister." I poked her in a stomach gently, and she giggled.

We walked inside, and there I put her down. As soon as her feet were on the ground, she ran to her father, who was still in bed, sleeping. She removed the blanket from his head and kissed his cheeks. Her father woke up, surprised, and kissed her back and played with her for a while. Finally, he came out from his bed and went outside to wash his face from the aluminum tank. When he stepped back inside, he dried his hands and face with a towel and put the towel over a hanger on the wall. Then he sat down on the bunk's foam mattress and my mom presented a breakfast tray in the middle of our gathering circle.

Kak Jalal said, "Bismela" By the name of the Lord, and start enjoying his breakfast, which was a cup of sweet tea with a sour cream and butter mixed with honey. We did the same, eating our breakfast. Each of us had a cup of tea and share the "nan" bread.

"When are you going back to the city?" Kak Jalal broking the silence.

"Soon, I guess," I replied casually.

"Like when? Today? Tomorrow or next week?" Kak Jalal demanded.

"As soon as I get ready," I said. "I'll wait until a car comes back to the village."

"But you don't have a key. How will you get in the house?" he asked me, slurping the remaining tea in his glass.

"I will break the door, I guess," I said sarcastically. "Can't you give me a key when I leave?"

"It depends," he said. "I mean, on your mom. Remember what I told you?" Kak Jalal put the empty glass down and got a sugar container to add few spoons to it; then he poured in some tea.

"Yeah, I remember," I replied.

"What's this all about, son? Going back to the city, a key, remembering what I told you—should I believe you're going to leave us?" Gullzar Khan asked suspiciously.

"Soon I will," I assured my mom. "And I believe you should know it, because I have told you already. I can't help anymore, Mom. I mean, this place is nice, but my patience is limited. You guys stay as long as you want. I can take a good care of myself. I don't need you watching after me. I am a grown man," I explained.

"Thank the Lord, you're a grown man," said my mom. "I know that, and that's the same reason I want you to stay with us, because we need you. I spent all those years serving you, and now, after all that, this is how you reward me? To run away from me and not listen? Nowadays, kids don't care what their parents say. At the beginning, I thought you were joking. I thought you just wanted to scare me, but you really mean it?" Gullzar Khan start sobbing.

"Yes, dear Mom, I really mean it," I said. "And I believe you understood me when I told you in the first place. After all, you've led your life all this years on your own, and you took care of me and rest of us. I don't know why you need me now." I was getting mad as I continued. "Besides, I am not vanishing forever. I am going to the city, not a battlefield. Whenever you need me, just send me a message and I will be here. Stop treating me like a little kid," I explained.

"I guess nothing is going to work with you," she said. "You didn't change your mind from what you decided, and I don't care what's going to happen to you." She stood up and went to the other room, coming back shortly with a little cup of honey and sitting down in her place. "But I want you to promise me that you will stay the way I taught you. Do you understand me, son?" Gulzar Khan announced.

"No, I don't get it. What did you teach me?" I asked her.

"See? I told you that you're not grown up yet, but you didn't believe me. Stay away from forbidden acts and know how to behave with your friends in public. I am afraid that anyone will tell you to do this or do that, and you'll just follow them without thinking. Nowadays, people change a lot, especially this generation. They all have gone crazy, they have no fear of anyone, and they don't respect their parents. most teenagers say (Don't talk about how it was in the old days, whatever past is in the past) but, my dear son, without looking at your past, you'll never be able to see the future. If you don't know where you came from and where you heading, you'll get lost. That's a rule of life on this planet. As they say, the one who doesn't have a past will never have a future," she advised me.

"I will have a future," I said, "if you let me try to find out for myself. You don't have to spoil me forever and never let me be myself and a grownup. Shouldn't I try to find out what I can become? Life is responsibility; I have to take this responsibility." I picked up my empty tea glass and washed it in the little plastic bucket in front of the aluminum tank of water that we have it in the room. "Mom, if I just work and eat, you tell me what's different between an animal and a human being?" I asked, trying to make her feel that I was grownup and knew how to talk.

"I understand what you're trying to say," she replied. "I'm not saying to stay that way forever. I am not spoiling you, but I want you work with my husband here."

"No, you don't, for sure," I said sarcastically.

"But we want to guide you through your life, like we did until now," she continued. "We're not worried about what you like to do, but if you follow your friends' advice—who knows? Maybe they'll try to put you in a trap. They'll see you with your family, that with Allah's help we have a farm, that we can do our business, and maybe they'll be jealous of what you have.." She tried to make me repent my decision. "On the other hand, maybe they can't afford what you can, and that's why they're asking you to be with them."

"Do you think my friends want me to be with them so that I'll spend money on them?" I interrupted.

"Who's going to run away from the beauty of nature and clean air and pure water?" She ignored my question and continued, "Now, in the city you can't stay comfortable, because it's hot and electric power goes off all day long, and there's not enough water to use. Also, a lot of foreigners come from all around the world. Who knows what type of human beings they are or what kind of diseases they carry." She was trying to scare me. "Besides, the city air is not clean like ours is in the village. There are too many cars causing a lot smoke, and there are a lot of diseases, and you are going back to live in a place like that? Oh, may God protect you, son. How will you survive? I don't know what would become of me if, God forbid, something terrible happened to you. Listen to me: following some friend's promise won't get you anywhere. If something happens, they will say that you chose to come along and take a position."

"I lived in the city for years and you never mentioned the black smoke and disease? Why now?" I asked. "Do you think I will be scared of what you tell me and change my mind? See, even now you are treating me like a kid. How am I supposed to grow up, Mom? Do you think I'm an idiot? You better stop forcing me to do what you want me to do. I'm going to find my way in life. That's the end of it. I don't want to hear any more of these arguments." I grimaced. "I will go, and you will see what's become of me. You should thank God that I don't say that I'm leaving the country, like all the teenagers who go to Europe," I informed her. "If I could afford to go to Europe, I wouldn't wait another minute. Do you understand?"

"I don't know what to say," she said in a desperate voice. "The only thing I know is that your friends turn your mind to evil. I ask Allah to protect you and bring you back to the straight path." She started cleaning the room and collecting the glasses and dishes. My stepfather didn't say a thing for all this time I didn't say anything elss and she keept quite.

After I finished breakfast I went outside to meet with villagers to find out when the truck will arrive from the city. After some chatting on my way to the farm, I found out it might be this afternoon. Some of their family members were planning to come back from the city, and usually, people come back around one or two o'clock on Fridays, which was today. Than I went to the farm to talk to Kak Jala, to let him know that I will leave, I went back home to grab my luggage. My mother was busy cooking lunch in the small kitchen. She came into the room when she heard my movement.

"What are you doing here?" she asked me.

"How much money do you have for now, Mom?" I asked, instead of answering her.

"Why do you need money, son?" she replied.

"You didn't answer my question," I said.

"Because first I want to know what you need money for," she repeated.

"In a few hours I will be leaving for the city. I went to the farm but I couldn't find your husband to let him know leaving. I'll go back after I get my stuff ready and have a few words with him before I leave," I said, looking around the room to think what else I shouldn't forget.

"But who you going to go with? Maybe the car or the truck won't arrive today."

"Yeah, they will," I said. "I will be leaving this afternoon. Do you have any messages for your brothers or sister?"

"God protect you, that's all I can say. You're not listening to us, and you've started getting crazy all of a sudden." She put her hands on her waist, looking suspicious about my sudden act of leaving, I saw from a corner of my eyes that she start weeping, she dried tears with her headscraf."

"Don't cry, Mom. Nothing's changing what I already decided," I informed her. "I'm leaving shortly, whenever the truck appears."

"May our Lord be displeased with whomever showed you this way." She started blaming my friend Hewa and beating her chest. "I don't know what son of a bitch misguided you—oh Lord, misguiding him, too." I keep it quiet; I knew nothing would stop her. "I guess you are your mother's misfortune. You are not listening to me. It's as if I'm your foe, but you listen to your friends."

"You don't understand me and are frightened of everything." I said

I left the house and closed the door behind me. As I walked through the narrow alley of the village, the odor of cows and sheep dirt in the air made me cover my nose and mouth. Finally, I spit phlegm out, clearing my throat. I thrust my hands in the pockets of my baggy pants, searching for the money. I took out some cash and calculated the amount in my head. I put it back in my pocket and kept moving along the road at a slow, steady pace, and thinking where my stepfather would be now. No doubt I needed more money than I had now.

Suddenly, a girl appeared, dressed in a long red gown and pink scarf. She was looking at me with a smile, and I looked back with pleasure in my eyes. Finally, I said hi to her, and she smiled and replied briefly "Hi" The sound of her voice echoed in my ear, like nice music. Sometimes when I walk through the forest in the middle of the day, I breathe a fresh, cool air. Her voice sounded like an echo of this air, and I breathed it deep down in my lungs. When she reached her house, she quickly went inside, but before she opened the door, she nodded her head toward me—this time with a big smile on her red lips. I smiled back, and her face brightened like a red rose in the pink scarf. Finally, she stepped inside and vanished from my sight.

I kept walking, looking back a few times with that hope of seeing her one more time before I left the area. I wondered what her name was and how old she was, but when she didn't come out of the house, I gave up and went on to where I suppose to go. I glanced at my electronic watch and saw it was 11:20—I recorded the time in my mind like a golden moment of my life. *At lunch, I will tell my mom, Gullzar Khan, that I'm sorry for getting angry with her, but I'm still leaving this afternoon*, I thought. *If I'm not satisfied there, I will come back later.* I continued walking toward the forest, this time at a faster pace, and soon, I vanished into the woods.

In the Sunshine Principal's Office

When the taxi reached the government official's alley, Zeno directed the driver to park in front of the house. The girls got out, and then the taxi left. There were two guards, Aras and Dyari, in front the house. Zeno asked Aras if the official was home. Aras replied yes. Of course, Aras knew Zeno because she had been in the house a few times. Then Zeno asked permission to go in, and Aras directed them inside and told them to wait in the living room. The girls sat on couches as they waited, and shortly afterward, the official came in. Deren and Sarah stood out of respect, but Zeno remained in her place.

"Welcome, guys," the official greeted them.

"Thank you," Sarah and Deren responded.

"How are you, honey?" he said to Zeno.

"I'm fine," Zeno responded.

"Would you guys like something to drink?" he asked.

"No, thanks," replied Sarah and Deren, but Zeno said nothing.

"What about you, sweetheart?" he asked Zeno.

"What about me?" Zeno said her attention was somewhere else

"Would you like something to drink?" he repeated with a smile.

"Yeah, I would," she replied.

"I will bring you a Coke," he said and turned to the kitchen. He ordered the chef, whose name was Hawzen, to bring Zeno a Coke with empty glass on a tray. Hawzen brought the Coke and placed it on the table close to Zeno. Then the official asked Hawzen to leave them.

"I don't like Coke," said Zeno.

"Then what do you like?" asked the official.

"I'm here to drink juice," she said with a smile, and Sarah and Deren giggled.

"Do you like orange juice?" the official inquired.

"No, I like your juice," she said frankly.

"It's here, honey. You can have it," he said with a smile.

Zeno stood and walked toward him. He relaxed himself in the couch. She kissed him on the mouth, then grabbed his zipper, undid it for him, and took his penis in her hands. He watched her with pleasure, then Sarah went over to join them. Deren froze in her place with fear and shame. Zeno left the official and went over to Deren. She kissed her on the mouth and helped her to take her clothes off. When both were naked, the official went over, and Zeno put Deren in position. She kissed her. "Don't worry; it's okay," said Zeno.

"She's just fine; that's normal," said the official. He grabbed her in his arms and started kissing her mouth, walking to the bedroom. Sarah and Zeno followed, then they closed the door behind them. He put Deren on the bed on her back. A half hour later, the sound of screaming reached the guards outside. They start to laugh.

Three hours passed. The house was quiet. The guards waited outside patiently; there was no trace of the girls.

"I wonder if they're staying here tonight," said Aras.

"It's possible," replied Dyari.

"I feel like a pimp in my skin," Aras said.

"Dear God, send a heart attack to this old buster," Dyari prayed.

"He will live longer than me and you," said Aras.

The living room door clicked opened, and Zeno came out. Sarah and Deren followed. They came down the stairs to the corridor and left the house. Aras and Dyari paid no attention to them. Shame and regret was clear in Deren's eyes, but it was too late. Zeno turned her face to glance at Aras and Dyari with smile; they smiled back and shook their heads.

The next morning, Zeno met Deren at the bus station close to their school. Then Zeno turned to Deren. "How did you feel?" she asked.

"About what?" Deren replied.

"About yesterday."

"I was a little bit worried," Deren replied.

"We all have that same feeling the first time," said Zeno. "It's normal to get that type of feeling, but then it goes away gradually."

"I'm worried because if my boyfriend finds out, he will kill me," said Deren. "I have to make him to believe that he's the one who lose my virginty, other wise he wouldn't get marriage with me"

"I didn't push you to do it," said Zeno. "You came of your own free will."

They walked in to the school and went to their history class. The teacher, St. Narmeen, had only just begun with details of the Ancient Roman invasion when the principal, St. Rwpak, knocked at the door.

"Yes, St. Rwpak?" said the history teacher. She turned to the class. "Everybody, stand up."

"Sorry to interrupt," St. Rwpak said. "I want Zeno in my office for few minutes, if you don't mind."

Zeno followed the principal, who didn't say anything until they reached the school office. Then St. Rwpak pulled out a desk drawer and took out a paper and handed it to Zeno. "I want you to give this letter to your mom, and I want her in my office tomorrow," said St. Rwpak.

"Can I ask what it's about?" Zeno asked.

"Your mother will find out when she comes here," replied St. Rwpak. "Now you can go back to your class."

When Zeno returned to class, Deren, who sat across from her, asked in a low voice, "What happened?"

"She wants my mother in the office," replied Zeno.

"What for?" Sarah, who sat with her at the same table, inquired.

"She didn't say," replied Zeno. "I will find out when my mother comes."

"Maybe it's about your grades," Deren imagined.

"That's what I think myself," said Zeno.

That day Zeno was little bit confused about the letter for her mother, because she knew that if her mother found out about her leaving school and that most of her grades were below the standard level, she would get in trouble with her mother. Then she got an idea. Because the principal didn't know her mother, Zeno thought she would ask Awaz, a woman who was a girlfriend and lover of the government official, to come to school and pretend she was her mother.

The Last Day in the Village

The air in the wood was cool. The water canals went through the woods, wind echoed through the leaves of the trees, and the chirping of birds mixed with a sound of frogs along the mountainside. The shade of the pine trees covered the ground, and I jumped over the water canals and stepped on the rocks in the water, The village folks used the rocks as a way to cross over to the other side of the canal. Finally, I reached the bottom of the mountain. I looked around for my stepfather, but there was not a trace of him. I roamed the area for a while until I found my stepfather's friend, cutting wood at the edge of the forest.

"How are you, Kak Rahman?" I shouted in the distance.

He raised his head and answered, "Oh, is that you, Rebeen? What are you doing here? I thought you already went off."

"Went off where?"

"To the city," he replied. He thrust his hand in his right pocket and took out a handkerchief to wipe his sweaty temple. "Weren't you supposed to go back this afternoon?"

"Yeah, I am," I replied. "But I'm here to see Kak Jalal before I leave. How can I find him?" I inquired.

"Why do you need Kak Jalal? Is there anything I can do?" said Kak Rahman generously.

"I just want to have a word with him before I go," I said.

"Is there anything wrong?" Kak Rahman asked me worriedly.

"Nope, not at all. I just want to say good-bye to him," I explained.

"He will be back soon," he said at last. "I guess if you wait a little longer, he will show up. Can you wait or are you in a hurry?" Kak Rahman inquired.

"I will wait. Where did he go anyway?"

"He went to the orchard," replied Kak Rahman.

"I will go there," I said, changing my mind.

"Okay, you have a good trip. Don't forget my messages to my family, and let them know I'm waiting here until they arrive," he said. "Tell them I'm fine; they don't have to worry about me. Tell them Rahman says he doesn't know why this time it took them so long to come back."

"I will" I replied.

"I don't know what they do in the city. It's so hot without electricity, as we all know," he complained. "I expected all of them here by now, to work with me. As you see, I'm short-handed. I can't handle all this work on my own."

I nodded to show him I understood.

"If you listen to me, son, you'll stay here with us. All your family is here, and they have a lot work to do. They need your help; you shouldn't disappoint them. Think about poor Kak Jalal," he advised me.

"I already did, but I've made my decisions. Sometime you have to sacrifice a little more to get what you want, am I right?" I asked the man.

"You sound like your father. May the Lord give you a long life, Rebeen Gyan " said Kak Rahman.

"God will reward you. See you in the city sometime soon, and for now I guess I'll just say good-bye."

"Good-bye," he said. "Take care."

I hastened my steps, running through the forest toward the orchard in the distance. Before reaching there, I saw him walking through the rows of the plants and collecting the produce in a basket. I ran until I got close to him. I was exhausted for a minute.

"What are you doing here?" I asked him.

He turned to me. "Is that you, son? What's going on?" replied Kak Jalal.

"I just came here to say good-bye. I will be off soon." I sighed. "I just was wondering if you need anything or have anything for me."

"No, I don't have anything. I'm fine," he said. "But did you get what I left for you with your mom?" Kak Jalal asked me.

"No, she didn't say anything," I said. "Like what?"

"Go ask your mom, son, and be careful. If you are uncomfortable in the city, you are welcome back any time you want. We're not mad at you," he assured me. "I don't know if you're mad at us, and I can't quite get it why you find it so hard to live here, while most people nowadays look forward to living in the village." He put the basket down and took a cigarette out in his pocket. "If anyone in that city full of people had a place in the village, they would run to it, because it's safer in almost every way, especially for someone like you." He sucked on the butt of his cigarette, dragging the smoke deep down into his lungs and then releasing the smoke from his nose without opening his mouth. "I wish you could find a way to go back to school. It's more beneficial than anything in the future. I better not take too much of your time. Come here, son, and give me a hug."

He hugged me and kissed me on both cheeks and wished me a good trip. I thanked him and promised him to try my best to be a good boy, and he patted my shoulder.

When I reached the village, I fixed my eyes on the girl's house with the hope of seeing her one more time, but this time, instead of her, her mother appeared at the door. I know her name, she's a friend of my mom, sometime I saw her accompnied my mom on their way back from the fountain, when they went to wash clothes or dishes. I heard my mom called her Shereen, but I didn't know that girl is her daughter, when first I saw her I said hi to Shereen Khan and asked if they had anything for the city; I explained that I would be leaving when the truck arrived. What I didn't expect to hear from her was what Shereen Khan replied: "No, thanks, son. May God be with you, because my daughter also will be leaving on the truck with you guys."

I could not believe what I'd just heard, but I was excited by the news. I went off, wondering if I'd get a chance to have some conversation with her daughter on the way, because most likely, she would sit in the truck by the driver, and I probably would be in the back of the truck. *But at least it's a good chance to get to know her name, or I can look at her more closely,* I thought with pleasure.

After I reached home I saw that my stuff had been placed by the door. I called to my mom, and she appeared shortly afterward with my youngest brother. He was naked from waist to foot—Mom had been about to change his pants. I bent down to kiss him on the cheek, and then kissed my mom's hand. "Forgive me for any discomfort I cost you," I said.

She kissed me back, chanting a pray for my farewell.

"I already talked to my uncle," I informed her. "He told me he had something for me with you. How much is it?"

"He told you he left something, not money. Why do you ask how much is it?" she said. "How do you know it's money?"

"It's supposed to be money; that's what I expect," I said. "Everything else I can get on my own. Don't make a fun of me. I don't have much time left!"

"Honey, I wish you'd change your mind and stay a little bit longer."

"Mom, this is not a good time for an argument. Don't worry about me anymore. I'm fine; this is not the end of the world," I complained.

"I guess for me it is," she said. "I've never lived apart from you. I'm not sure if I can manage my life without you around." She start sobbing.

"Mom, if you love me, you have to support me. You have to give me a chance to know myself and practice my ability. Life is too short, and I don't want to miss this opportunity, even though I know this job doesn't satisfy my needs. But still, it's a new experience for me."

A neighbor outside announced that a truck had arrived. I grabbed my luggage, and my mom hand me some money. I hurried to the white Toyota truck that was stopped a few yards from our house. The villagers who had arrived from the city jumped out from the back of the truck, and those who were traveling to the city, like me, gathered around the truck.

I looked around for the girl, but she was nowhere to be found. Finally, she appeared at the other end of the alley. I didn't recognize her at first, because now she was dressed like a city girl, wearing blue jeans with a silky white sweater. She was wearing dark red lipstick and the mascara on her eyelashes that brightened her beautiful dark eyes. Her bright face glowed in the afternoon sunlight as she dropped her luggage in the back of truck. She got into the truck, next to the driver's seat, but when Haji Ali, the truck driver, saw her there, he said, "I'm sorry, sister. You're supposed to sit in the back. An elderly couple will be with us, and they'll be sitting up here."

She didn't complain; she just got out and moved to the back of the truck. She sat across from me and at first, she didn't look at my face or say anything. She started chatting with the women who were sitting near her. I listened to their conversation and learned that one of her companions' names was Zyan. I talked with other male travelers in the truck about daily work in the farm, but I was thinking, *What is her name? Why doesn't she have any interest in me when I am available for her? Why won't she even say hi, like she did the other morning?* I couldn't stop thinking, but I came to the conclusion that it was because we weren't alone, as we were the other morning. I had to find out where she was planning to live in the city. I thought, *Love is so strange—you fall in love with someone at a first glance sometimes, but what's hidden behind those eyes that are capturing my attention?*

Then I heard the crying of a little boy, who happened to be her little brother. Her mother was coming toward the truck, holding the boy's hand. When she saw them, she shouted to her mom, "What's going on? Why is he crying?"

"I don't know what happened. He says he wasn't to come along with you. No matter how hard I try, I can't keep him quiet," she complained. "I told him that next week I'm going to the city and will take him with me, but he didn't stop crying. I think it's better if you take him with you now."

"Don't worry, Mom, I'll take care of him. Come here, sweetie."

The little boy opened his arms and ran toward the truck. The other women around the truck grabbed him and handed him to her; she pulled him up by hands.

"Don't cry, Hardy," she said to the boy, "If you cry, I won't take you with me, okay?"

When the truck started moving, and the boy was assured that she wasn't going to leave him or drop him off in truck, he finally calmed down. His face was covered with dust over his dried tears. I took a piece of candy from my pocket and held it out for him, and she sent him toward me. "Go get that candy, Hardy," she said. He smiled and stepped forward to get the candy in my hand, but I took him by the hand and held him in my arms and started playing with him. I kissed his cheeks and helped him to open wrapped candy. He put it in his mouth and munched on it. I said, "Kiss me on the cheek," and he did.

She directed her brother, "Say thank you," and he thanked me with a shy look on his face.

The village disappeared from sight after the truck turned onto the narrow road that led to the main road toward the other villages. I asked Hardy why he liked to go back to the city, but he didn't answer. Instead, he stared at the cuff of my shirt and tried to unbutton it. I asked him, "Where are you living in the city?" But he was not old enough to remember the name of the area. She replied, "Say 'Baranan.'" Hardy repeated the name with a smile for me. That's what I wanted to find out. At the first stop in the city, we dropped off the elderly couple, and at the next stop, other travelers got off. She remained, along with a woman and her companion, and Hardy and me. The driver, Haji Ali, asked me, "Is it okay if I drop them first at their homes?"

Instantly I replied, "Yes, I am fine with that." I was looking forward to this opportunity so I could find out where she lived.

Then the driver said, "One of you can come to the front if you want to."

She said to her companion, Zyan, "If you want to sit in front, go ahead, please." Zyan hurried to sit by the driver, and we remained where we were. Now I had the chance to tell her what was on my mind. "Why did you decide to come back to the city?" I began. "I mean, is there any particular reason for that?"

"Of course," she replied. "I'm going back to school, but my mom will remain in the village little longer. How about you?"

"I have a job waiting for me here. I quit school a few years ago and don't have a permanent job, but maybe I will stay with this job if I like it."

"What kind of job is it?" she asked shyly.

"As a guard with some government official. One of my dear friends works with him," I informed her.

"That's fine with me," she said. "But it's better for you if you had finished your school."

"Oh, thank you," I said. "You don't mind if I say something?"

"Like what?" she asked with a smile on her face.

"Like ... I like you," I said. "I believe you've noticed that."

"I like you, too," she responded with shyness. "I guess you already know that." Her face flushed as she spoke the words until her skin was quite pink.

"Yeah, I can tell by looking at your face." I said "But I mean something greater than just 'like.'" I watched her to see how she would react, but she said nothing. After a while, I finally I said, "I am in love with you! I love you!"

She didn't respond or say anything, but her face blushed more every minute. She turned her face to the front so the air could blow in her face, and the smell of her perfume mixed with air we breathed. I said nothing else; I was afraid of upsetting her. I waited a little longer, but she didn't respond. When we reached her house and the truck stopped in front of the house, she jumped out and gripped her brother's hand. I helped to take out her luggage, and finally she turned to face me and said, "I feel precisely the same way you do."

What I ashamed most at the moment, until than I wasn't able to bring myself to ask what's her name, I was so excited when I heard her say that. I bent down to kiss the little brother's cheeks and found another piece of candy for him. I asked Hardy, "What's her name?"

He put the candy in his little pocket and replied, "Her name's Talar. Why don't you know her name?"

"Now I know," I replied. "Thank you. You guys have a good day."

She smiled and said good-bye to me. I couldn't take my eyes off her. The truck driver asked me to sit in front, now that he was alone, but I refused to go. I fixed my eyes on Talar and Hardy until the truck made a right turn from the alley and I could no longer see them. After the last glance, I closed my eyes, hoping that her image would remain with me forever. And the last words she said "I feel precisely the same way you do" echoed in my ears until I reached home.

The Story of Zeno and Her Family

Zeno was seventeen years old and had two little brothers, ages eight and nine, and a little sister, seven. Her father died when Zeno was eleven from tuberculosis, and her mother decided to sell the house about five years after her husband died. The house had four bedrooms and a kitchen and a small garden. They sold the house and bought another smaller house in a different area. Her mother had no income and no outside job, as she'd been a housewife when her husband was alive. Zeno's father had a tailor with a small shop in the city market, and after he died, Zeno's mother sold the shop but kept his sewing machine so that she could start a business at home.

One of their new neighbors was also a widow, but she didn't have any children; her name was Awaz. She rented a room on the second floor in the home of the Karem family, who lived in a two-story house. the Karem family also have another room on the same floor, but Karem used it for his own staff, and he kept the door locked.

Awaz also had no income. She lost most of her family in the war and decided to get a job somewhere as a secretary. That's what Awaz promised Karem when she rented the room from him, so Karem decided to help her because she had a little education. She finished middle school, but when she was applied for secretarial position the board of education office, she was directed to get a letter of recommendation from a government official. A colleague directed her to that government official, and he gave her the recommendation letter right away. He also told her that when she got the job, she should visit him, and she obeyed because she appreciated his help.

After her first week of work, she went to his house. She knew that he was married, but she still hoped that he might want to marry her. He was very attracted to Awaz at their first meeting. Awaz had a very sexy body, and she knew that, so that day, she wore her best suit, beautiful makeup, and a very nice fragrance. The taxi dropped her off in front of the official's house. Two guards were standing outside the house, and after she told them about her visit, one of the guards went in to get permission for her.

When she got in the house, the official saw her and was impressed. "Welcome, welcome," said the government official, leading her a couch in the living room. She wore a light red shirt with a black skirt to the knee. She wore no stockings, so her beautiful skin was exposed, and the smell of her fragrance filled the living room instantly.

They sat in silence for few minutes, and then the official, M, began, "How's work?"

"It's very nice. I appreciate your help," Awaz replied. "So how are you doing?"

"I'm doing fine," said M. "Is there anything else I can do for you?" he offered

"No, thanks," Awaz replied. "I'm here on your request of the other day to visit you after I got the job."

"I remember very well," said M. "We will see each other more often from now on." Awaz said nothing but smiled shyly. "Today is your day off, I guess?" said M.

"Yes, that's why I'm here," Awaz replied.

"I believe you are single,"

"Yes, I am," Awaz replied with pleasure.

"You never got married?" M inquired.

"I was married once, but my husband was killed in an accident," said Awaz.

"I'm sorry to hear that," said M. "What did he do for a living ?"

"He was self-employed, building houses," Awaz informed him.

"So how he was killed?" asked M.

"One of his co-workers dropped a block from the roof by mistake. It hit him on the head, and he died instantly."

"How long did it happen?" asked M.

"Almost four years ago," replied Awaz.

"So why haven't you remarried?" M asked.

"I don't know," Awaz replied. "Only one guy asked me, but somehow I wasn't in the mood to marry, so I refused him."

"Do you have any kids?" M inquired.

"No, I don't."

"If I asked you to marry me, what would you say?" M asked with a smile.

"I don't know," Awaz replied shyly.

"Say yes or no," said M. "It's as simple as that."

"I don't know," Awaz repeated.

Then M stood up and got closer to her. He sat beside her and put his arm around her shoulders. "Don't be shy," he said, and without her permission, he turn her head toward him and kissed her on the mouth. They kissed for some time, and then he put his hand on her breasts and gently stroked them. A few minutes later, she was in his arms, walking toward the bedroom.

When he reached the bedroom, he put her down on the bed, slowly taking off her clothes, piece by piece. Soon, they both were naked and making love.

Their relationship began like that. Awaz spent every weekend at his house. Five months passed, and then one day, M told her that his wife, who lived with his children in Europe, found out about their relationship. She would apply for divorce if he wanted to marry Awaz. Awaz asked if M was willing to marry her. Of course, the deceiving official, who just wanted to have fun with her, replied no. His reason was that he had eight kids with his wife and didn't think divorcing her was a solution.

Awaz showed no regret, but she was afraid that if she made M mad, he would fire her from her job as a secretary or disgrace her in the public

The official, M, said, "I heard from someone that they saw you with a teenage girl in the market last week."

"Who saw me?" asked Awaz. "And what does that have to do with you?"

"It's no matter who saw you," said M, "but I want to know who that girl was. You said that you don't have any children and have no relatives in the city."

"She's my neighbor's daughter. Are you satisfied now?" Awaz retorted.

"So you have a friend?" M inquired.

"Yes, I have. Do you think it's something strange?"

"No, not at all," M replied "I wonder if you can bring her with you sometimes."

"What do you mean by that?" Awaz inquired.

"I mean to spend some time with her here," M said frankly.

"You mean in the bed?" Awaz inquired.

"In the bed, in the living room …" M said.

"You're old enough to be her father!" Awaz informed him. "Are you crazy?"

"Maybe I am," said M.

"I don't think I can do that," Awaz said. "And she's a virgin, I should warn you."

"That's fine," replied M. "You were a virgin, too, once."

"But are you going to marry her?" Awaz asked.

"I can't say that," replied M. Then he went on, "But look, I might willing to get married to you, and we can share her sometimes. Didn't you say you like women, too, while we were in bed?"

"But you already have a wife," said Awaz. "Also, you want to keep her. What if she finds out?"

"If you promise me to bring her with you next time, I can promise you we will get married," said M, deceiving her.

"What about your wife?" Awaz inquired.

"I can get rid of her any time I want," said M. "Didn't I tell you she's four years older than me?"

M didn't forgot that when he was in the mountain twenty five years ago, the girl he wanted to get marriage with, her family refused to give their daughter hand in marriage to him, because he wasn't able to have a house, and he was a solider who wasn't able to resided because of the nature of work he was involve with, five years later, when he meet his wife now, he got marriage with, even though she's four years older than him, but he was doubted that he could find a wife anytime soon, so simply he accepted what the fortune brought on his way, but he was desired for a younger one, this feeling of revenge live with him for rest of his life.

"Really?"

"Of course," M assured her.

"Let me see what can I do," said Awaz.

First Evening in the City

The truck stopped in front of my house. I took out my luggage and paid the driver. I unlocked the door to the house and went inside, carrying my luggage to the guestroom.

I took a quik look around the house, than changed my clothes and shaved my beard, I decided to take a nap for couple hours, after I woken, I put on a short sleeve lime-green shirt, with a pair of black pants, brashed my hair, put some clogne then went out.

I thought about Talar and little conversation we had in the car earlier. I pictured her in my mind, standing by me now, hand in hand. She would say that she likes the smell of my fragrance, I imagined, and I would thank her. I pictured her with a smile on her face as she told me "I am in love with you" a few hours ago.

The sun would set within the next two hours. "I'd better catch Hewa before dark," I told myself. "I'll check his house to see if he's home by any chance."

I went out through the narrow alley toward his home. When I reached his house, a little boy was playing with a small toy with his friends; he seemed to be Hewa's little brother. When I asked if Hewa was home, the little boy replied, "No, he's not at home."

"Is your mom home?" I asked him.

"Yes, she's home. I'll get her for you."

The little boy ran inside and called his mother. Shortly, a woman appeared wearing a white headscarf and a long blue gown with long sleeves.

"How are you, Mom?" I said when she faced me.

"What can I do for you?" she replied with respect.

"I am here to see Hewa. I'm a friend of his. My name is Rebeen," I said. "I just came back from the village a couple of hours ago. Hewa sent me a letter last week and mentioned that maybe a position was available for me at his workplace. I'm looking forward to taking it because I have been looking for a job for a long time. Last summer, around June, I went back to our village with my family. I spent the last three months on the farm. Now I am tired of the village and was looking for a reason to come back to the city. I was really happy to get in touch with Hewa when he sent the letter last week. I just told my mom I was returning to the city, so here I am."

She hesitated for a moment and then said, "Oh, may the Lord protect you, son, with my Hewa. He's at work now, but he will be here tonight. I will let him know you were here," she assured me. "Do you have a cell phone number? I can tell him to call you if you have one."

"No, I don't have a cell phone yet," I said. "Does he have one? I will call him myself."

She held up her hand. "He has a cell phone, but I'm an illiterate woman. I don't really remember his number." She smiled. "If you have a telephone number, write it down for me and I will give it to him to call you when he comes home."

"I don't have a home phone either," I said. "Just let him know I was here. He can visit me at my home. He knows where I live. I'm not very far from here. Thank you for your time, and good-bye."

"Good-bye, son. I will let him know," she replied.

I walked through other alley toward the bazaar of the city, through the crowds of people, sellers calling out for the merchants on the streets. The echoing market area was like a buzzing beehive. I roamed around and finally found myself in front of a cell phone shop in the market. I entered the shop to look at the phones, but I left the shop without asking any questions, as the owner was busy with other customers. I continued walking from shop to shop, wandering around. Not much had changed in the marketplace, same old same old, except for those cell phone shops. When I reached a grocery store I bought one kilo of tomatoes and six eggs, along with some leeks, celery, green onion, and cucumbers.

After roaming around the market for another half hour, I turned around and went home to make something to eat for supper. As I walked, I saw teenagers in groups, standing by the sidewalk. Most of them watched the girls walking by, looking at each of them from head to toe. Some were in very sexy dresses, and the young boys uttered a few words to describe their beauty, but those females walked on without paying any attention to their words.

Sometimes, the boys followed a girl until they got a chance to talk to her. When they got a chance, they linked their body from behind to her body or moved a hand over her buttocks in a quick move. Some girls seemed to enjoy that, but the innocent girls increased their paces to escape the area.

I decided to stop at a teahouse for a drink of tea before going home, and I overheard a man telling a story to his friends.

"Nowadays, our life style change because of all the changes in the country, a lot of prostitution organizations spread around the country," said the man. "Some of them rent a house somewhere or buy it, and they open a whorehouse. Now and then, they are caught by the security teams in the city, when people start to complain to the government and give information about the places and locations. Sometimes the newspapers print a story about government officials also involved in this, but they usually come out innocent in front of the folks. Some of those prostitutes in the interview have been questioned in the weekly newspapers, and they assure us that they've slept with many high-ranking officials in exchange for a great amount of money," the man went on. His friends nodded in silence. "Everyone know when those prostitutes are caught and charged, the government let them go free, but once again, they start all over in another location—just like a mushroom that comes out from nowhere. One of the prostitute said in the interview, "Because I am beautiful and young, I slept with many government officials in the last six months. They send for me very often."

The man continued the story as his friends slurped another tea. "I read this in the newspaper the other day" said the man and went on "On the other hand, one of the sluts said she started this business six years ago, when she was fifteen. She said, "My mom found it hard to go on living because we had no income, until one day a rich old man came along, and my mom handed me to this old guy in exchange for money. The man took me to the capital city for the first time. I was so scared of all the violence and car bombings I heard, but he took me to a house in a narrow alley of the capital city. He left me alone for some hours, and when he came back, he asked me to go with him for a walk. Finally, I found myself in front a of bigger house, bigger than the one the old man lived in. I thought that this man was my husband, because my mom mentioned it to me when she handed me over to him, He knocked on the door of the other house, and a young man about twenty-five years old opened the door and welcomed us. I thought he was this man's son. He smiled at me and looked delighted. When I stepped inside, I saw three other men seated on couches, drinking alcohol and watching a TV. Women in bikinis were sitting among them. By the atmosphere in the room, I realized that I had become a prostitute. I tried to run, but they got me and pushed me in the bedroom by force.

'They were seven men. I had no idea what was waiting for me. On my first night, four men came to me, taking off all my clothes and rubbing me all over. One of them took out his penis and filled my mouth with it. The other one started with my anus from the back; soon all my holes were filled. I vomited on the floor, but they never stopped. I have never experienced that harmful, wild, bothering act before. The blood gushed out from my body. I lost my virginity that night. The man I expected to be my husband turned out to be a pimp in the capital city. He was pimping for others who looked to have some pleasure, who were looking to satisfy their wild desires. That night I was bleeding so much, and the following day I got sick and spent most of the day in the bed, out of fear and pain. Those animals accosted me the night before. I tried to escape but I was too young. I didn't even understand the language they spoke. I was cried for hours under my blanket. I hate my mom for what she did to me. I'll never forgive her. Sometime I even wonder if she was my real mother or some stranger who claimed to be my mom. I never met my father; she said that he was taken by the special guard of a former regime one night when I was still a baby. She told me that my father was executed for some crime he never committed—the reason was that he refused to go to a birthday party for the dictator in the company where he was worked. One week after the birthday party, they took him out from his bed in his pajamas and bare feet. She never saw him again after that. Almost nine months later, they called her and gave my father's corpse to her.'" The man finished the story to his friends in the teahouse, while I decided to pay my bill and head home.

By the time I reached home it was dark and the electric power was off in the alley. When I get close to my house I could see that someone sat by the door. He stood up and looked toward me. Because it was dark, I was not able to see his face clearly, but when I get closer, I could see that it was Hewa,

"How are you, Rebeen Geyan?" he asked as we embraced each other. "I missed you so much. I am glad to see you! My mom was told me you came to my house."

"Yeah, I came around this afternoon," I said. "I am glad to see you, too, buddy."

"Welcome back. Look at you—your color changed. I guess that stepfather of yours treated you like a soldier in the army. You're pale man! You should get some rest. I think you deserve it, don't you?" said Hewa with smile.

"Yeah, sure I do. I miss it here so much, but it wasn't too bad in the village. It's fun, like a vacation," I explained. "Your mom said you were at work tonight."

"No, I had a day off and went out with some of my friends today."

"Well, we have plenty of time to talk," I said.

"Did you bring back anything from the village?" Hewa asked.

"Let's get inside first and sit down. I'll make something for supper, then I will tell you," I assured him.

We went inside, and I took out a lighter that I always carry in my pocket. I clicked it on, lighting our way to the living room. There, on a small table, was an oil lamp. I remove the safeguard glass, lit the lamp, and then put the glass back on.

"You guys don't have electric power through the public line?" Hewa asked.

"No, we don't," I said. "I'm the only one here, Why would I want it?"

"You're right; I shouldn't ask. Anyway, let us go back to our story."

"What story?" I asked.

"Your story in the village," Hewa said. "Did you get any girl in your village? And how's work? You spent the last three months there—your summer vacation without me. Of course, you had the homemade bread and all the delicious dairy with honey from the honeycomb. Did you bring me any souvenir?" Hewa asked with a smile.

"Sit down and relax," I told him. "I'll fix something to eat, and later on, you will get something to take home, too."

"You mean like honey, or homemade cheese, or butter, or some fruit?" Hewa asked.

"That's what I said. You didn't eat yet, did you?" I asked Hewa.

"No, I didn't, but I'm not that hungry," Hewa replied.

"Come on—you have to eat with me, no matter what. Are you shy?"

"Shy to you? I don't think so. I am not a female, shy to you."

"You have to prove it," I said, "and you wrong. Nowadays, females are not shy like they used to be."

"No, they aren't," he agreed. "I will eat a little bit with you. I ate lunch about two o'clock in the restaurant with a friend of mine; that's why I am not hungry. I know you are tired. You must have gotten up early this morning to catch a car back here," Hewa guessed.

"Home? You better say 'to the city.' My mom calls the village home, not here," I informed him.

"But I am talking to you, not your mom, and I believe you call it home, not a city. Am I right?" Hewa asked.

"I guess so. And I did wake up early but not to catch the car; to catch Talar, my sweetheart, and also from happiness that I was coming back home."

"You got a girl?"

"Yeah, just today," I replied.

Hewa asked no further questions. I started washing the tomatoes in the sink while he watched.than I chopped tomatoes in the plate, I took out the fry pan, add some vegetable oil in to the pan, I also chopped some onion mixed them together with three eggs, fried them on the gas stove, when its got ready we shared together

"It was strange," I told him. "When I saw her on the truck with me, our hearts pounded for each other. Our love is real."

"Man, I can tell," said Hewa.

"Yeah, I love her truly. Anyway, I wasn't sure if the truck would arrive today, but I'm here now and that's all that matters," I said.

"Yes, but the position already has been taken by someone else," Hewa teased.

"You're kidding me! Don't say that!"

He burst out with a big laugh. "I'm just joking. It's still waiting for you, and that's why I came this evening—to make sure you are prepared for tomorrow morning." He hesitated for a moment, then asked, "Do you have a gun handy?"

"No, I don't," I said. "Are we going to war right away?"

"No, we are not," he replied, "but how can you call yourself a guard without a rifle?"

"We have two guns in the village, but neither is mine, and my stepfather didn't want to give me one to use because my mom disagreed with my being a guard."

"I see," Hewa said.

"I know that I need a gun, but that's why I didn't ask him," I explained.

"Don't worry. I can get you one until you can find one for yourself," said Hewa.

"So, tell me about the job and schedule," I urged him.

"It's easy," said Hewa, "as long as we don't have a terrorism attack."

"You have been attacked in the past?" I inquired.

"No, all prays for the Lord of heaven, but you never know. When you carry a gun, you have to be prepared for all sorts of possibilities, especially with a government official. This is a matter of life or death." He paused for a moment. "I want to be honest with you. Frankly speaking, if you don't feel comfortable with the job, no one is pushing you to do so. I'm just trying to help." He stared at the ground, searching for words. "I don't want your family to think I offered you this job to get you in trouble. It's your choice. I've done this job for a year now. A lot of people became policemen because they get paid good, but this job pays more than what they make, so you will, too. I don't want to scare you away, but nowadays, nothings is guaranteed. At the same time, could something happen today that would cost me my life? Who knows?" Hewa waited for me to respond.

"I know that's true," I said. "But where is the location, and you didn't tell me about the schedule and our day off during the week."

"You need a job; don't worry about a day off," Hewa advised me. "If it's necessary, you can take a day off when you want." He paused for a moment and scratched the back of his neck. "Anyway, I will take you to the place tomorrow. It's located in the northeast, a nice area in a huge house, you're going to get lost in it!" Hewa try to cheer me a little, but I hesitated for a moment.

"Oh, did you guard his house or his office?" I asked.

"It doesn't matter," he replied. "We're all over, wherever he's want us to be."

"How many guards are there?" I inquired.

"Depends. It changes all the time. But always at least two of us stay in the house, and I would say we're around fifteen guards, beside his drivers and three in the car with him," Hewa explained.

"What type of cars does he have?" I asked.

"One Chevy Suburban, and a Mercedes, and a Toyota 4Runer," replied Hewa,

"What are his drivers' names?" I asked.

"Oh, you don't need the drivers' name."

"I just like to know," I replied.

"I don't know their names. Why do you want to know?"

"I heard something about one of them," I said.

"What did you hear?" Hewa inquired.

"I heard that people see the guy who drives the Mercedes every week with a bunch of high school girls in the car. It's rumored that he has sex with them in the house. Did you ever see any girls?"

"To be honest with you, I haven't seen anything like that," Hewa assured me. "As far as I know, that's just a rumor."

My voice grew husky. "That's not what I meant. I just heard that someone said it; that's why I asked you." I cleared my throat and spit out phlegm into the sink, then turned on the faucet to drain it down. "But what about others, like a woman?"

"What do you mean?"

"I mean not young girls but women, you know, like whores," I explained,

"Yeah, I see some women." He smiled. "But I don't know if they're whores. After all, his son also lives with him, And his wife and other children live in Europe, so that's why I don't know for sure."

"What do those women look like?" I inquired.

"I don't know; they're women. What did you mean?" asked Hewa.

"I mean are they young? How old are they?"

"Old enough. Maybe about his age. I mean, the one who comes more often."

"So there is a 'one.' I thought he was trying to hide something from me, Do you know her name?" I asked.

"How should I know? She doesn't talk to me, but most of the time I see her in the Mercedes." His face had a look that indicated he couldn't quite find the right words. "So she gets out in the garage and goes inside, and after about two or three hours, she leaves again. She might be that type that folks talk about it, but I don't know for sure. Why? What did you hear about young girls?"

"Oh, nothing, just forget it." I tried not to talk about it when I saw he was uncomfortable with my question.

"Come on; are you hiding things from me?" said Hewa. "I'm not going to tell what you say. Don't you trust me?"

"That's not the question." I tried to explain myself. "The thing is, I've heard from one guy that a few girls in one high school are around there. I guess they have been seen by people in one of his cars." I tried to find a short way to tell him. "And what they said about those girls is not good, you know what I mean?"

"Yeah, I understand, but how people can see them in the car with its darkened windows? And why we should care about him sleeping with that woman? It's not my business."

"But people saw those girls while the Mercedes was in front of the house," I tried clarify the question.

"You mean they've been in the house?" Hewa asked. He didn't seem to understand me.

"Yes, they were; that's what I heard," I replied.

"I don't understand what you mean. I've never seen any high school girls around. He doesn't have any of his girls here; they're all in Europe."

"Well, maybe they're wrong. You know people tell all kind of things." I tried to end the subject.

"But I don't know if they come during those days I'm not working," he said after giving it some thought.

"Maybe it's possible," I agreed.

Hewa thought for a minute, taking in what I'd said. He seemed to consider something, and then he said, "I believe when he takes the woman home, he always comes back one hour later or more. I think she lets him do it, too, in her home, or on the way there. Or maybe she lives somewhere far from here." Hewa seemed to want to feed me more information.

"So you don't know where she lives?" I inquired.

"I never follow them," Hewa explained.

"So what about his family—his wife and daughters?" I inquired.

"What about them? Didn't I tell you that they live in Europe? Who knows? Maybe they're doing the same thing. What goes around comes around, as the saying goes.

"How many kids does he have?" I asked.

"I don't know; I wasn't a midwife," he replied sarcastically. "But I heard that his older son studied for his doctorate in Great Britain in political science at Oxford. Nowadays, everyone is going crazy. Everyone is looking for three things," said Hewa.

"What are those three things?" I inquired.

"You don't know?" he went on. "Power, money, and women. When you have power, you can make money, and when you make money, you can have as many as women you want, when you have no fear of God in your heart," Hewa explained.

"I agree that's true," I said. "It's a strange world."

"Actually the world is not strange," said Hewa. "We're strangers in this world. We think we will live forever without paying any attention to our future. Everyone wants to have this world to himself. Everyone deserves to have a power and a lot of money, so when we have all this, we look for more and more. That's why all the dictators in the world seek power. When you have power, you can have many things. That's a rule. After all, the dictators in the world will eventually die like everybody else. That's why no one should think he is greater or better than someone else. We all are born equally, but we do not live equally. Finally, we all die."

"Death it's a great punishment for ignorance," I said, "for those one who think this life is the final destination. But death and the aftermath of death puts a period on their happiness. Nowadays, everything is turned upside down, especially in our region. You have to let it to be that way until it fixes itself or until it's destroyed once and for all, like an ancient place."

"We're not about to change anything here, no matter that people do whatever they like," said Hewa. "So we chose not put our noses in anyone's business. We're just leading a poor life now." He sighed. "Believe me, those type of rumors we hear on a daily basis could turn black hair to white. That's the reason I like to have friends like you. I wouldn't trust most of the guys I work with. They're nice, but I still have to be aware. You never know; see what I mean?"

"Yes, I understand what you mean." I said. "But why don't you just quit the job? If he sleeps with a different woman every night and you're guarding his ass, there's no difference between this job and a pimp," I explained. Hewa nodding in silence, so I went on. "You stayed out there in the rain and snow, and he's fucking all kind of cunts inside, delivered to his door."

"Well, that's his home, not mine or yours. After all, anyone can sleep with whores. You simply pay them. They're like a bathroom—everyone uses it. But still, for someone in his position, it's a shame," said Hewa.

"I know what you mean, but why doesn't he bring his wife back home from Europe if he's so hungry for sex? If I had a wife and family, why would I look for something that has less value? This is nonsense to me, but of course, that's not what he thinks."

"His wife is old and dry. Those that he sleeps with all have a fresh cunt, thirty or thirty-two years old. I am sure if he get the youngest one, he will not let her escape from his dirty hands. He's hungry; he will fuck anyone he can get his hands on; anyone sitting in his lap," Hewa explained.

"Should I be afraid that one night he'll call me, too?" I said sarcastically. "What are you going to do? When he's in the mood and getting hard, will he call you in?" We both laughed.

"He can get the smoothest thighs and wet holes. He doesn't care for a guy like me. We're like goats, while he can get all those clean-shaved cunts. Why would he dirty his cock in the shit of my ass?" said Hewa.

"Why don't we get gals like him? What's wrong with us?" I inquired.

"Were you looking for some, too?" asked Hewa surprisingly.

"No, I am just kidding," I replied.

"Even if you really wanted to get a woman, you have to be rich like him. After all, you still need a pimp to pimp for you, like the one he has, or you have to hunt for yourself. This type of business needs experience; it's not that simple," Hewa explained. "I guess for us, it's better to just fuck the devil in our dreams—I mean, the wet dreams."

"Who's finding whores for him?" I inquired.

"I'm sure he has a pimp. There are a lot out there nowadays," Hewa replied.

"I mean, do you know the one he has?" I inquired.

"No, but just by looking at the faces of the women who visit him, I can tell why they're there. After all, you can see right away how they walk—their legs are more open, like they carrying something between their thighs. Also, if you see anyone like that, look at her lipstick. When she comes out, you'll see the change."

"What change you can find in their lipstick?" I inquired.

"It's just like they came out of a cosmetic shop. They have new makeup, and most of them carry lipstick in their purse. They put on some when they finish, before they come out, but sometimes they forget and just wipe their mouths."

"Wiping their mouths?" I asked, confused "From what?"

"The special juice he serves them inside, the milky juice," Hewa laughed.

"Oh, really?" I said, amazed how Hewa describing it, as if he watched them while they're engaged in their action "How do you know that?"

"How do I know? It's simple. The truth is that everyone knows M works, eats, and fucks. Everyone knows his behavior around the women. If one night he sleeps with his clothes on, that night must have some kind of danger in the air."

"Who said that?" I inquired.

"The other guards, who have worked with him longer than I have. I'm sorry; I guess you still don't believe me, and I can't videotape it for you."

"Did you ever see him naked?" I inquired.

"No, but I saw him in his underwear in the living room. Don't you believe me?"

"Yes, I believe you, but did you say at first that it was only a rumor?" I inquired.

"Because I want you to take the job and not regret it," said Hewa. "I was afraid you'd change your mind and leave the job. I want you to know that a few guys came over to get the position, but I asked our leader to put it on hold for you, until you returned from the village. You understand now?"

"Thank you for your kindness. I sincerely appreciate your friendship," I said, "but you should've told me about this in the first place."

Hewa tried to console me. "But that is not our business. I guess we can't make any changes."

We finished dinner, and I washed the dishes.

"Would you like to go to a movie tomorrow?" Hewa asked.

"Sounds good. Where should we meet?" I said.

"In the main square, by the booksellers on the sidewalk," Hewa explained. Then he sighed. "I am a little tired, and I just don't feel well. Maybe I'm getting sick. I'd better be going."

I gave Hewa some honey and butter with some natural chewing gum our villagers collecting them from some trees and went through different prosses bfore sent it to the market, and then I escorted him to the door. He thanked me, and we said good-bye.

In the Morning

I got up at 8:00 AM the next day, washed my hands and face over the sink, and then went to the kitchen to fill the kettle and put it on the gas stove to boil for making tea. I filled a cup with sour cream and placed it and a box of butter and some cheese on an aluminum tray. I heard the bread seller in the alley, shouting, "Hot bread!" I stepped out to the alley and called to the boy. I bought four hot loaves of bread, then stepped back inside, locking the door behind me. Back in the kitchen I grabbed the sugar cup on the countertop and got a glass. I poured myself some tea and sat on the foam mattress, enjoying my breakfast.

Later, as I was about to go out, Hewa called me.

"Are you awake?" Hewa asked me.

"I just finished my breakfast and am on my way out."

"Why don't you come down to my house?" Hewa suggested.

I agreed and was soon on my way. I stopped at a small shop to buy two cigarettes, lighting one of them and puffing the smoke out of my nose. Two high school girls walked past me. I glanced at on my watch 9:15 a.m. I imagined it was late for them to be going to school; I thought they should be in class by now. When they passed by me, I turned around to watch them from behind. They were beautiful, although they paid no attention to me.

A few minutes later, I reached Hewa's place. I held my hand up to knock on the door when the door cracked open, and Hewa stood in front of me.

"You almost hit my face!" Hewa teased. "Don't break my nose first thing in the morning!"

I smiled at him. "Good morning! Let's walk to the market."

"We will," he assured me, "but first let me call a guy. I have to pay him a visit."

"What guy?" I inquired.

"A friend of mine," he replied. "He lives close by. First, though, I have to see if he's still home. Let me call him first." He took out his cell phone and keyed the number, and after few rings, Hewa said, "How are you, Kak Bakhtear? Are you home now?" Hewa nodded at me to show that his friend was at home. "I have a favor to ask—do you still have your rifle? I wonder if I could borrow it from you for a month or so." Bakhtear said something to Hewa, and then Hewa responded, "I still have mine, but I'm going to give it to a dear friend of mine. He needs it for a while until he buys one, so I want to borrow yours, if it's possible." Bakhtear again said something to Hewa, to which Hewa responded, "I really appreciate it. It wouldn't be for too long, I promise. Can I come there now to get it?" Hewa nodded at me again and said into his phone, "I'm on my way."

Hewa put the phone away with smile on his face. "I got you a rifle. Of course, you will be using mine until you buy one; I'm using his."

"Thank you for your help. I don't know how to pay you back for your kindness."

"With a butter and honey from the village!" Hewa said.

We chuckled at that and started walking to his friend's house. In another alley, located behind Hewa's house, was a two-story building with a light gray Nissan Maxima parked in front the house. Hewa walked up and rang the doorbell. We waited for few seconds, and then I reminded Hewa that the power off at this time of day. He then knocked on the door, and shortly afterward, a man who I supposed was Bakhtear opened the door. He was still wearing his pajamas.

"Sorry to cause you too much trouble," said Hewa.

"No trouble at all; don't worry," said Kak Bakhtear. "Please come in. Let me grab the for you,"

"I'm really sorry to cause you trouble," said Hewa.

"Don't repeat that; anything for you," said Kak Bakhtear as he went to the back of the house. Shortly, he reappeared with a rifle in his hand. "Here it is," he said, handing it to Hewa.

"I appreciate it," said Hewa.

"It's fully loaded with bullets," said Kak Bakhtear.

"Hopefully, we won't need to use them," said Hewa.

"Hopefully not," said Kak Bakhtear.

"Thank you for your help and kindness," Hewa said.

"Any time," said Bakhtear.

"We'd better be going. I want to take him there—maybe he can start working today."

"So the rifle is for him?" Kak Bakhtear asked.

"No, I'll use it myself and give him mine," Hewa explained.

"I'm glad to hear that," said Kak Bakhtear.

"Good-bye now," we both said.

"Good-bye, guys."

Hewa hung the rifle on his shoulder and we walked toward the city center, where we would catch a bus. The bus not ready to leave when we boarded it; we wait for other five minutes until four passengers came to fill the empty seats. Finally, we were on our way, heading toward the alley, and when we turned the corner, the house came into view. It was a big house, and two guards were seated on chairs in front of it. "That's Kak Aras and Kak Sardar," said Hewa.

We got off the bus and approached the guards.

"Welcome, Kak Hewa," they said in greeting.

"Is Kak Awat here?" Hewa asked them.

"I believe he's inside," replied Sardar. "Why do you come so early today?"

"I want to see Kak Awat," Hewa replied. "I want to talk to him about my friend." He pointed to me. "This is my friend Rebeen. He wants to work with us, if Kak Awat will hire him."

"Welcome, brother" said Aras.

"Welcome to the board," said Sardar.

"Thank you," I said.

"Let me call him out," said Hewa. "You wait here; I will be back."

Hewa walked inside, and Kak Sardar turned to me and said, "What are you doing now, Kak Rebeen?"

"I don't have a job," I replied. "I was in the village last summer. I just came back yesterday."

"How's the farming this year?" Kak Aras asked.

"Not bad," I replied. "We grew some tomatoes and zucchini and eggplant."

"So you like the village life?" Aras inquired.

"I do," I replied, "but only in the summer. I don't like it there in winter."

Hewa came out with a guy who looked to be about twice our age. I supposed he was Kak Awat.

"This is Kak Rebeen," said Hewa, introducing me to him.

"Nice to meet you," I responded.

"Welcome to the board," he said. "I'm Awat, by the way, and I'm in charge of the guards here."

"Hewa told me about it," I informed him. "I'm glad to working with you guys."

"You seem like you're ready to start today," Awat said.

"Yes, of course. Hewa got me this rifle today. I appreciate this opportunity," I said to Kak Awat.

"You are welcome," said Kak Awat. "Just leave your rifle in the guards room, and we'll see you this evening."

Hewa escorted me to the guards room, where there were three beds, a small refrigerator, and a satellite TV that was playing the news. When we left the room, I learned that the government official wasn't home at the time, so I didn't get to meet him. Later that evening, I would come back to start my new job.

In the Government Official's House

"Remember when you told me about the girlish-looking driver of our boss?" Hewa asked me. "You said people saw him with girls in the car—high school girls, judging by their uniforms."

"Why? Did you see him, too? Mother fucker! I'm sure he told the girl that it was his own car, and she believed him."

"He had *two* girls in the car," Hewa corrected me. "One sat in front, covering her face with a book, and holding up her hand by her face so she wouldn't be seen."

"I wonder how many times she was sucking him on that seat?"

"Too many times, I guess" said Hewa.

"I wish one day his boss would find out or see him while he's driving those girls around. Then he'd get fired," I said.

"I don't think his boss would him for that," Hewa informed me, "because he knows how many women his boss has slept with. I am sure he knows their cell phone numbers and even addresses."

"So tell me now," I said, "when I told you in the first place that your boss is a master fucker, that people see what he does, why did you say it was a rumor. Why did you try to hide this from me?" I inquired.

"I know the boss slept with whores and that his driver took her home after they were done," said Hewa. "I guess after the boss finished, he also did it at her home later, but I don't know about the high school girls that you said were in his car. Maybe it was the driver's girlfriend," said Hewa.

"Anything is possible these days," I agreed.

"Honor left our community long ago. For the sake of money, they sell their bodies and honor and everything else. This generation is the craziest generation I have ever seen in my life. My father says it all the time, when I ask him why he doesn't buy a cell phone for himself. He makes fun of me and says that when he was my age, when he would travel from the village to the city, he drove only his number eleven."

"What do you mean, number eleven? Is that his license plate number?" I asked.

"His legs," said Hewa. "He walked—no car or horse. He never had a driver's license in his life, and doesn't know how to drive at all, but I believe he knows how to ride a horse or donkey; that's all he knows." Hewa chuckled.

"I know. But what does that have to do with a cell phone?" I inquired.

"He said a cell phone makes you lazy. It makes you to refuse to go see your brother, sister, father, or mother. You just say, 'I don't have to go see them; I will call them on my cell phone,' so gradually, you forget them, and the love you have for them will be gone before you know it," Hewa explained. "That's the way he thinks."

"Yeah, he's right," I said. "That's another bad effect cell phones have. I don't blame him." I hesitated for a moment, then said, "Today, everyone tries to fill their pockets full of money, and it doesn't matter how they get it. They will get what they want and find the whores to fuck. Nowadays, everywhere in the country you can get whores, if you really look for them. Besides, some teenagers have gone crazy, and no doubt communications has a big role in it. But who's responsible for all the wildness?"

"Of course, the government and the law," Hewa said after some hesitation.

"Mercy of the Lord be upon you; that's true," I said. "The government and the government officials—they're the ones who bring all those whores business to our country. If they're captured and punished, they will stop, but as we can see, just for the sake of the media and news, they say we've captured some groups from here and there, but after a short period, they let them all free." I stood up and hung my rifle on my shoulder. "They will start up all over from another corner, under a different name, and you know what? If you go to stores that sell women clothes, you will find female teenagers at least once every day. They are willing to suck store owners for perfume, or a shirt, or anything. They take them into the fitting room at the back," I explained to Hewa, who nodded in response. "It's a horrible world we're in. Only God can protect us from all those misbehaving in the community. Have you seen how they talk about ADIS in the media and warn folks to protect themselves from it? Why? Because they know what's going on and what a mess they made. They brought ill behavior to the new generation, but on the other hand, they are warning us to protect ourselves from those diseases. That's God's punishment, sending it to human beings."

"AIDS came from the unusual sex, and the virus sprouted before you knew it!" Hewa said.

"I know it came from unusual sex with other creatures, like animals. That's what I heard," I explained. "But the thing is, when you take a wrong way, God punishes you however he wants, and he has all kinds of punishments."

"Don't you see nowadays that they bring women from other countries to work in their houses? I mean, those businessmen who bring merchandise from other countries. They also bring women from those poor countries, and they start raping them in their homes," Hewa explained. "Also, there are some offices around the city, and you can go there and ask for a worker, and they'll order one for you. Frankly, they're importing human beings for work, but later, they do other things."

"That's the first time I've heard a thing like that," I said, surprised. "We hardly make changes in our lives, but we're all guilty about what's happened in our community. But the problem is that no one listens or hears us. If I get a chance to put you down, I will do so. No doubt that is how we behave with each other."

"Really? That's what you have in mind?" said Hewa, sarcastically.

"No, we're friends. But for example, if you tell someone to pray a daily prayer five times, God protects you from a major sin. They say, 'If I don't want to do something, I just don't do it.' They don't know that if you go away from God, the devil will invite you, or when someone tells women to cover themselves because the Lord orders them to do so, they say it's their right to do whatever they want, or they say you're against feminism or human rights. But if you let them be a whore, like we've seen with our own eyes, freely looking for customers on the streets and trapping teenagers here and there, that's their right, and you shouldn't bother them," I explained.

"I guess everyone's looking for fresh cunts nowadays, and teenagers have what they looking for, but we're not looking for those things. That's why we don't get it—it's that simple," said Hewa.

"You reminded me of something," I said. "I have a friend who owns a jewelry shop. He told me that one day, a teenage girl came to his shop, asking for the price of earrings. He told her all the prices. and finally she asked my friend, 'What about a free one?' And my friend said he asked her. 'Where can you get a free piece of gold?' She said, 'I don't know. Maybe if you want me, I will do you whatever you like, if you have a room.' My friend didn't understand at first, but she repeated herself a few times until he understood. That's when he told her to get out of the shop right away."

"Yeah, they're all over," Hewa agreed.

The car appear from the corner of the alley, that's him the driver of our boss "See, look at that way," I said, and Hewa turned his head. "He's come back. How ridiculous he is. Just like we're his servants, he has no shame. It's so rude, just like we're a wall or a rock. Who you think you are son of a bitch you're just a M's pimp we all know that" I said

"He's not hearing you, why you bother?" said Hewa

"He doesn't even look at us," I went on. "We'd better put him in a trap and break his face. Did you see his narrow, ugly face? It's like the shape of my penis. When I see him, I remember my cock. When I take a pee, I see his face and his mouth like my pee hole." We both laughed.

"Why do you hate him so badly?" Hewa inquired.

"I just can't help myself when I see people like that arrogance, ingnorance, disrepectful. Did you notice how he tilted his head to other side, as if we're invisible?"

"I agree, but we are both going to lose our jobs if we put him in a trap. Just wear him like your shoes—don't even think about him. It's not worth it," said Hewa.

"Trust me, I would like to see a donkey's face every day but not his face. He thinks he's so important, finding himself beside his boss. Fuck, you're a pimp. Who do you think you are?" I said.

"Let's not waste our time by talking about someone we don't like," Hewa suggested. "Tell me, is your mother or stepfather asking you to go back to the village yet?"

"No, why do you ask?" I replied, surprised.

"I just wondered," replied Hewa. "And I was wondering if you missed your sweetheart."

"Don't you remember? I told you; she came back here, too," I reminding him. "She has a school to go to, until next summer."

"So that means you will be leaving us next summer?" he inquired.

"I don't know. Maybe. But since that day, I haven't had a chance to talk to her. I'd better find a reason to go to her house and see how she's doing."

"You'd better go soon, or you'll lose her. You have to talk to her, face to face."

"Yeah, but I have a little fear that she's not ready for that yet," I said. I glanced away as I searched for the right words. "Besides, if someone sees us together, it won't bet good for either of us. I'm afraid things will get worse if I talk to her— people will get the wrong idea if they see us on the street."

"Everyone is doing it," Hewa insisted. "Why do you care? I mean, you could talk to her on her way to school, just a friendly way of talking, without saying anything about the subject this time. Even if she's with a female companion, it doesn't matter. You're a relative or family friend—who cares? You can't wait forever to tell her what's in your heart, and she's not waiting for you forever. If you don't show a positive action toward her, she'll go to someone else, and you will lose her."

"Will you help me?" I asked. "Tell me what should I do. As you said, I might lose her."

"I will, but you don't have to have a fear of talking to her first," Hewa warned me. "Whenever you see her, talk to her right away, like you're talking to anybody else you know—just in a normal way, like, 'Hi, how are you? How's you father?' or things like that. Ask about her family, and she will answer you, of course. Then gradually, you can get closer to her, until it's a habit for both of you. You told me she's aware that you're in love with her, so she understands the reason. After all, you'd better make sure she notices it. When you get a chance to see her alone, tell her how you feel about her. See if she's still interested in you, because you said you can tell that she loves you by her behavior, right?"

"That's true," I replied. "She said she is."

"But also make sure not gave it too much space of time, if you're not discussing the matter with her, she might think that you're playing around. After a few times, open the conversation and she will tell you, if she intresting you, and from there, the door will open more further so you can make up your mind. I mean, do you really want to marry her? If you see any difficulty right now, you'd better back off." He seemed to search for words. "Because if that's not going to happen, don't waste your time or hers. If you're not sure that's the outcome, you'd better back off. That's my advice, but the choice is always yours."

"Did you ever fall in love with someone? Do you have any girlfriends at all? Do you have experience? I know she loves me."

It took sometime for Hewa to reply, he shook his head, than he facing the other direction, when he turned back to me . "I haven't had a chance to have one, like you. I have experienced a difficult life," Hewa said. "I've had a lot to deal with in my life, and it's too early to think about girls or married life. I have a desire for girls as much as you do, don't get me wrong, but I am not going to carry a heavy load on my back that I might not be able to lift from the ground. You know what I mean?" Hewa inquired.

"Yeah, I know what you mean."

"So it's up to you," Hewa said. "Maybe I am wrong about what I just told you—you're free to do what you want. I am just advising you not fall in love or get trapped by love. Nowadays, we can't be sure about most of the female companions. The freedom of our country brings a lot of strange actions from here and there. Too many things are going on at once," he went on. "Nowadays, you hear that close friends or relatives don't care for each other like they used to do in the old days. My father, for example, hasn't gone to his brother's house for almost three years now."

I nodded. "I have hard time understanding things since I met Talar I thought, she's totally occupying my mind. Everything has changed to a wrong direction in this country" Hewa went on. "The cities are full of strangers, and people are busy making money. Everyone opens his mouth and is talking about companies and businesses," . "Everything we do is for the sake of filling our pockets with money, and it doesn't matter how we get it. That's why I'm trying to not lose her, because I know her and her family well," I explained.

"Well, good luck to you then. Go talk to her tomorrow on her way to school, and don't let that opportunity pass by. Life only gives you one chance. Tell her what's in your heart and see what's going to happen," Hewa advised me.

Just then, Sardar came toward us. "Guys, be prepared. We are going to go out to the meeting held in Kalachwalan," he informed us. "Maybe take us five to seven hours, but we'll all come back here before morning."

"We're ready whenever they wish to go," said Hewa.

Before too long, the government official came out; he was talking to someone on his cell phone and seemed as if he'd just eaten, as he was using a toothpick to clean food from his teeth. Everyone jumped into the cars, and one of the guards opened the back door of the Mercedes for him. They all left, leaving only three guards in the house.

Today, for the first time, I went along with Hewa and the government official on duty.

The Night of the Meeting

We were on the way to Kalachwalan for an urgent meeting. All three cars were on the road, one after another. Hewa and I were in the Toyota 4Runner. The driver, Rebwar, was alone with Sardar in front; we sat in the back.

"Were you guys in the house this afternoon?" Rebwar asked us.

"No, we were there last night," replied Hewa.

"Why do you ask?" I inquired.

"His girlfriends were there," Rebwar informed us. "They were watching a movie."

Sardar laughed out loud. "I heard them scream in pleasure."

"Are you serious?" Hewa interrupted.

"Of course I am," Sardar said. "One of them said, 'Please don't push it too hard.'"

"Oh, God, it really is a whorehouse," I said.

"He said, 'Don't swallow it; just wash your mouth with it,'" said Rebwar.

"Oh, it's disgusting. I'm going to throw up. Stop!" said Hewa. "So, what happened then?"

"They got a taxi and left," Sardar replied.

"He didn't offer to take them home?" I inquired,

"Why would he do that? After all, if I drove them home, their family would ask, 'Who's this guy?' Or 'Where have you been?'"

"Does their mothers know?" I inquired.

"How would I know?" said Rebwar "but I doubt it, if anyone know their daughter involved in such activity, I mean prostitution, they will kill them" Rebwar explained.

It shouldn't be there.

"I don't understand why M not bringing his wife back from Europe," I said, "or how his children don't say anything."

"What children? That's his only son that he has here," Rebwar interrupted. "He's really a nice guy—very respectful, and he doesn't know what his father is doing."

"What about his wife?" I asked "Do you think she's doing same in Europe as her husband is doing here?"

"Those types of people like our boss for example are so lucky, they get hand on whatever they please," said Sardar. "I know a man with a nice wife and kids and quite a good job, but he has a relationship with a woman—she's married with children, but her husband is dumb. He goes to work every day, while she goes out to meet her boyfriend."

"Maybe they're related somehow," Hewa suggested. "Or maybe he's her brother."

"No, he's not related to her. Why would she meet her brother every day?" Sardar disagreed.

"This city of ours is full of whores and pimps nowadays," I said. "Before we know it, we'll be strangers in our city, because we're not engaging in this."

The car bumped on the lumpy surface of the road, and Hewa and I moved unsteadily in the back, holding our guns. The government official had a meeting with other commanders in the fortress in Kalachwalan. The plan was to send more armed forces to the front lines of the war, for the freedom operation in the other part of the country. This government official was in charge of part of northern army force, so the meeting was important, For that reason, the official went back and force almost every other day. By the time we reached Kalachwalan, other commanders already were sitting in the meeting room, waiting for him to arrive. In front of the fortress office, their guards roamed around and their cars were parked all over the place. The secretary of defense also attended the meeting.

The government official went in alone, and we waited outside. After two hours of negotiations, he came out, and we drove back to the city without any speaking. On the way back, he made a short stop for a rest in the teahouse at the bottom of the mountains. Then he told his drivers to drive for Kara Hanjer instead going home, even though it was about ten o'clock. The drivers followed his order, and we reached the place before midnight. When he was finished with his business, we headed back home. It was about 6:00 AM when we finally returned, and the other guards were wandering around in front of the house when we arrived.

The Day after the Meeting

The car parked in front of the fancy garage door. The rear door opened and the government official stepped out. The driver behind the wheel was the one who hunted girls on the way to school. Hewa and I hated him so much. After he killed the engine and took the key from the ignition, he got out of the car, locked the doors, and followed his boss into the house without saying a word.

The other guards asked Hewa and me where we'd been all night.

"He was in the meeting, of course, and we waited in the car and talked, telling jokes all night long. It was fun but I'm sleepy now," replied Hewa, yawning.

"Go get some sleep, then," one of the three said.

"I will, as soon as I find out if we're going home," said Hewa.

"Why don't they you go home after a night of traveling?" said another guard.

The guard leader came out of the house and announced that the government official had gone to sleep so we could go home and come back the next evening. Hewa asked the guard leader if he could take today and tomorrow off—he needed to take his mother to the doctor—and he received permission for that.

Soon, Rebwar drove us home and we chatted in the car. "It was a long night. It could have been horrible if we hadn't had companions. I wonder how some people can spend a night without anyone to chat with," I said.

"It's easy: sleep," Hewa answered me.

"I mean to be a guard during the night, which requires that you don't sleep," I explained.

"Come on; how could one be a guard with a weapon, alone at night in someone's home, especially a government official?" said Rebwar. "And it would get boring, like you said. After all, this is not safe for him, either."

"I meant someone who was guarding on the streets during the night. I know it's impossible to leave a house like that, but I am talking about loneliness, when you're left alone, just like no one cares for you. You know what I mean?"

"Yeah, I know what you mean," replied Rebwar.

Hewa started laughing and said, "Don't be afraid to go ahead and visit her in her house, Find an excuse. Why should you be afraid of someone you love? She will be surprised to find you at her front door, and I guarantee she will love you more. Don't even think twice; just go get her."

"I will!" I said.

"Oh, he's talking about that kind of loneliness. Now I get it," said Rebwar.

"Don't worry about me. Tell me: do you need any help taking your mother to the doctor?" I offered.

"No, thanks, we'll be fine, and thank you for your concern. I think I will take her to the specialist, not just a regular doctor. Specialists pay more attention because of the extra money they charge."

We reached Hewa's house by that time, and I said, "I pray for her. God make it easy, giving her quick recovery, and don't forget, any time you need my help, just give me a call. I will be there."

"Thank you so much. I appreciate your concern," said Hewa.

The vehicle started moving now; only Rebwar and I remained inside. When we came to a gas station, Rebwar stopped for gas, and I went inside the shop to buy a pack of L&M's with a lighter. I came back out at the time that Rebwar was paying for the gas. We both got in the car, and I lit a cigarette. I rolled down the window, blowing the smoke out, and shortly, we reached my house.

I went inside and put the gun in its safety position. Then, after making sure all my doors were closed, I put on a pair of pajamas, got in bed, and soon was snoring.

The Day We Discover
Some Evidence

Hewa and I were at the bus station, and when the bus arrived, we got on and looked for two empty seats that were side by side. I sat down and put my rifle between my legs and held it with my right hand. We watched through the window as people walked around on the busy street. Students came back from school—some alone, some in a groups—with books in their hands. We noticed a school bus full of girls and thought that the driver had a good job.

"He's a lucky guy, I guess," I said. "Would you want to trade your job for his him?"

"I would," replied Hewa. "But I'd guess he wouldn't like that exchange. If I was him, I wouldn't do it either." He giggled. "He's a king behind his wheel, He listens to music and enjoys chatting with those nice gals." I didn't make any comment so he continued. "Whatever, we shouldn't bother. By the way, will you do anything this afternoon while I am with my mom?" Hewa inquired.

I sighed. "I don't know. It depends on my mood. Maybe I'll go to Shab's teahouse. I have some friends that I used to see before I went to the village. We'd meet at the teahouse almost every afternoon and chat for hours, playing dominoes on the table."

"Well, enjoy your afternoon, but don't forget you have to go back tomorrow evening. And be careful because I'm not going to be there. Don't fall asleep. Be extra cautious. And do me a favor—if anyone asks you why I'm taking off today, don't tell them, okay? This is just between you and me."

"Don't they know your mother is sick and that's why you're taking two days off?"

"That's one reason, but in reality, I have a different plan for tomorrow," said Hewa.

"A plan?" I said, confused. "You didn't tell me anything. I don't know what you are talking about."

"Just forget about it—it's not very important," Hewa said.

"Come on—are you hiding things from me?"

"This is just between you and me, but I'm afraid you will accidentally mention it to someone," said Hewa.

"You're not going to tell me?" I raised my eyebrows. "I thought you trusted me," I said sadly.

"No, I didn't mean that. You're not taking it seriously, are you?" said Hewa. I said nothing and he continued. "I will tell you, but promise me you won't tell anyone at all. Promise?"

"Yes, I promise," I said. "What is that big secret?"

By this time, the bus had reached another station and some of the passengers got off the bus. Hewa waited until they had passed us and then said, "The truth is that I'm tired of this job and found a new one. I will be leaving soon; that's my secret."

"Did you want quit this job? I get it now—that's why you sent me a letter. You want me to take your place, but guess what? If you quit, I will quit, too, And I don't care what you say. You have to find a job for me in the same place that you found a job. I came back from the village because of you!"

"Well, I haven't been offered the job yet—I'm not sure of they will hire me. And I'm not leaving until I find out for sure, so you don't have to worry for now, okay?"

"Well, I do worry. I know what's on your mind."

"What's on my mind?" Hewa asked.

"You're tired of this motherfucker, of his behavior, of those whores he brings home. It makes you feel like a pimp, so you want to escape. You brought me here so they would let you go. That's a big trap and you are using me," I retorted.

"You are right that I want to quit, but trust me, that's only one reason, not all the reasons. But if this new job hires me, I will tell them about you, too."

"You will if you're really my friend. Remember, you sent me a letter when there was a position available, and now you are trying to leave me. If you don't find me a job with yours, I will never talk to you again," I complained.

"We are more than friends ;we're like brothers, so don't worry," Hewa assured me.

The bus stopped when it reached another station, and some passengers were dropped off. We were dropped off when we reached the government official's area, and we walked to the house, where two of our friends were sitting on the chairs outside, drinking warm tea. One of them had a cigarette in his hand and was puffing the smoke out through his nose and mouth.

"Good morning, Kak Brwa" we greeted him.

"Good morning, young men," replied Brwa. The other guy went back in the house when someone called him from inside. "Seems like you're up early this morning. You still have another thirty-five minutes before you start work. What makes you guys wake up so early? Do you have some other business to take care of?" He drank the remaining tea in the glass. "What school did you attend before you came here? Are they beautiful?" Brwa teased,

"No, that's not what we're up to. We didn't have girls or school to attend " I said, and Hewa went inside.

"I don't buy it" Brwa said with smile. "You guys deserve it. Everybody has one nowadays. I have one myself. What's holding you back from that?" He looked at me in a friendly way.

"We deserve it, too, as you said, but nowadays, everything's going upside down. You have to be very careful to pick the right person and not fall in a trap," I explained.

Brwa put his teacup on the cement bench, took another cigarette, and lit it with his green plastic lighter. He puffed the smoke out. "I agreed with you" he said "you should look for a bad person but someone who's nice and you can count on. I believe if you really want it, you will get one, don't you think?"

"I don't really try because at this time, I don't have that process in my mind. I can't afford it—you know everything needs money, and I don't have enough of it. My salary isn't enough for me to save anything. It's too much trouble, so I'd better forget about getting married. Am I right?"

Brwa tilted his head. "I can't say I disagree with you, but you don't have to hold your hopes aside and not try it. If you wait until things change, you might waste much of your time in waiting. You should do something before you have no time left," Brwa advised me.

"We never know what will become of us by evening," I replied. "It might be that we will never see each other again. Death always is out there for us. I don't say I'm not trying to live a life that everyone else desires to have. You are married, if I heard correctly, right?"

"Yes, that's right, and I have a daughter, nine months old."

"God give her a long life with mercy," I praised him.

"And give you a nice family with kids, too," Brwa praised me back.

"You always have to be very careful about which person you chose, as every day, hundred of couples apply for divorce and end up with regret. Some of them even have kids, so that's another problem," I said. "Women nowadays are crazy; I mean, they don't want to listen to their husbands. We know our nature as men, and when we get mad at them, we divorce them. It's unfortunate for both. You have to be aware of all of that before you enter the process. It's just a headache, that's all."

"So do you have one in your mind at all?" Brwa asked.

"I do, but it's kind of difficult," I said. "There are a lot of things to take care of in my life, and I am not the only one in this country who has so much to think about it. There are millions of others like me in this country, and most of us don't know what will become of us or our future." I pulled up a chair and sat beside him after I hung my rifle by the wall. "People are busy collecting wealth, and they forget all other aspects in their lives. If you have money, you can buy anything you want. Whatever it is, you name it. But without money, without a home, without a permanent job, making a family in this country might be a big mistake that you will regret later." I crossed my legs and put my hands behind my head, relaxing. "Speaking of regret, I have a dear friend who recently got engaged. They were immediately attracted to each other, had a brief courtship, and then got engaged. Now he couldn't find a place to live, either the rent is too high he's not afforded, or what he afford he couldn't get it, his fiancee's father said, if they didn't getting marry in two months, the marriage would be off, the poor guy frustrated, the girl's family already has pushed him to spend a lot of money on gold, let the engagment party coast they had asid. Now I'm in trap, he said the other day, unless her family support him, or give him more time until he servive from the situation. He won't be able to marry, and he doubt it that her father will change his mind.

"It's a crazy world," said Brwa. "Do you have that kind of problem?"

"Who doesn't? If we had another house, I wouldn't worry, but we just have one house here, and there are seven in my household with me. I don't want to add another person to my household. I should get my own place, but there are no other options to choose. Besides, we'd still have to buy furniture and everything else, from a needle to a TV and bedroom furniture—you name it," I explained.

"That is true, and of course everyone needs that. You have to be ready for it, and after a while comes a kid and buying milk and diapers. And then they get sick and there are other expenses. Are you ready for all that?" Brwa inquired.

"I guess I'm not" I chuckled.

"I can see it in your eyes, and the back of your neck is wide—you can carry a big load, like I do." We both burst out in a big laugh.

Suddenly, Hewa came out of the house, picked up his rifle and put it on his shoulder. Then he popped some sunflower seeds into his mouth individually and spit out the shells.

Brwa watched him for some time. "You'll have to sweep it yourself later. Don't make a mess," Brwa warned Hewa.

"I will, Kak Brwa, don't worry," Hewa replied. "Would you like some?" Hewa offered a handful to us, and we enjoyed them together for a while. Brwa took out his cell phone and called his wife. Finally, he stood up and walked a few steps away from us for some private talk with his wife. At last, he closed the phone and came back to his chair.

"Do you guys know the price of battle gas now?" Brwa inquired.

"I guess about six dollars. Did you sweetheart ask you to buy some?" Hewa teased.

"Of course, she asked, women ask a lot from their husband. You better stay single; listen to my advice," said Brwa.

"Think twice before making any decision and you won't regret it later. Besides, no one knows what God has in store for us," said Hewa. "After all, I am not the one who is looking for a wife. You know who is?" Hewa asked, pointing at me.

"Precisely, that's what I agree with. Who knows what God has in store for us, and also, I am sure you heard that it's a good deed if you get married. For example, in religion, we learn we should do it quickly," I said.

"Are you up to getting married right now?" Brwa inquired, facing Hewa.

"No, I am not, but I know someone who likes to hear things like that" Hewa looked at me and chuckled.

"Oh, congratulations, I didn't know the bridegroom was sitting beside me," said Brwa. "So when are you arranging the party? I like a party and dancing. Will you invite us?"

I knew he was teasing me. "Yeah, I will, but it's a long way from now. Hewa just wants to make fun of me because he doesn't believe in love or relationships, I guess," I said. "Simply, he's not in love, that's why."

"Are you talking about me? I do believe in relationships if I could get lucky like you, but the thing is, I'm not ready like you are now," Hewa explained.

"What do you mean by 'now'?" asked Brwa. "Like tonight?" They started laughing.

"Whatever," I said, getting upset. "I'd better not tell you anything. You can't keep a secret; you just spread it around."

"Why are you upset?" said Hewa. "I didn't tell Brwa anything. You just told him yourself, right here, right now." I just looked at him without a word. "But he's a nice guy," Hewa said, "and I'm sure he won't tell anyone. He's one of us. After all, you're serious about it."

I turned my face in the other direction and looked at the tree growing along the side of the house. Finally, I asked, "What tree is that?"

"It's just a green tree. It doesn't produce anything. I guess it's just for shade and beauty," replied Brwa.

"He just wants to change the subject. He's shy when we talk about his affair," Hewa said, chuckling.

"Oh, I see what you mean," said Brwa.

"He's a village boy. How could he not know what kind of tree this?" said Hewa. "He knows better than we do, but he pretends not to know it."

"You don't have to be shy," Brwa announced. "Men shouldn't be shy in front of men. Nowadays, not even women are shy. Don't you see our boss every week, opening a fresh virgin cunt?"

"You're kidding. Who says that?" inquiring Hewa.

"I'm not kidding, but maybe you've been sleeping, or you didn't chance to see them until now," Brwa said.

"Did you see them?" I inquired.

"Only few times," replied Brwa. "Not that I saw them doing it, but I saw them when they arrived here."

"I told you so," I said to Hewa. "You said it was a lie, that folks like to make up stories. Maybe you'll believe me from now on."

"Okay, expertise boy," said Hewa, "skilled investigator, I know he's sleeping with a woman, but I never saw any teenagers."

"That's because you're not here when they arrive on Thursday afternoon. He takes them in for four hours or five sometimes. I can hear them screaming inside, especially those who lose their virginity," explained Brwa. "He's also going to fuck a nice boy, too, if any are around. He's very lusty man, just seeing a hole to put his penis inside." He put his hand in his pocket and touched his penis through it to flatten it down so it wouldn't not appear in his pants.

"Man, you get horny when you talk about it," I said. "See? He's hiding his things from us. You already have a wife. That should have happened to us, not you." We were chuckling.

"You're just teenagers. You don't have any experience. Whenever we talk about it, you get hard like a rock," Brwa informed us.

"If you feel uncomfortable, you can just go to the bathroom now and relax yourself, because you have to be here for another ten hours. Besides, we're not going to stop it here. We halfway grasped the conclusion of the subject," Hewa advised him.

"Go fuck yourself. I'm a man. I can control myself, not like you. You just see a little sexy body on the street, and you run to the bathroom for a hand job. And you keep thinking about it in bed until finally you end up with wet dream." Brwa was getting upset.

"That's natural; everyone's going to have a wet dreams before they get married, so why are you blaming me?" asked Hewa.

"Don't talk about that fucking subject any more. If you want to have sex, go get married or find a whore and pay a little and they'll satisfy you," said Brwa.

"Did you fuck any of these girls that your boss is sleeping with? Those high school girls you talked about it?" Hewa inquired.

"They all belong to your boss. He's the one who's pricking them off, one after another," Brwa explained. "Besides, I didn't say they were school girls. How did you know?"

"I know anyhow; that's not a problem," replied Hewa. "But how did you know all that? Seems like you know a lot about them. Did you pimp for him or what?" Hewa wanted to give him a hard time.

"You are really rude. You're losing your mind." Brwa got mad. "If you had minimum respect, you wouldn't utter words like that to my face. I'm not a pimp, and you'd better watch what your mouth is spitting out. Brwa grimaced.

"Don't get mad; I'm just kidding. I'd just like to know a little more about them. I know you have more information than I do, right?" said Hewa, trying to calm him down.

"Why do you want to find out? What for? To check if your sister is among them?" Brwa chuckled as if he'd gotten even.

"Fuck you! I have no sister in high school to worry about. Maybe you have one. I just want to see them." Hewa grimaced. "I might try them some day," he confessed, not knowing what to say.

"*You*?" Brwa scoffed. "I thought you were somehow a respectful person, but I guess I was wrong. If your boss gets a chance, he'll also fuck you too, not only nice little seventeen- or eighteen-year-old gals."

Hewa didn't give any reply to this; he just faced the opposite direction and then finally asked, "Anyway, how long have you been married?"

"I have been married for almost two years. Why? What do you want to know?" Brwa inquired.

"How long have you worked here?" Hewa asked instead of answering Brwa's questions.

"About seven years," replied Brwa. "Why all the stupid questions about it?"

"And how old are you now?"

"He's like a doctor who's checking with the patient about symptoms," Brwa said, looking at me. "I'm twenty four."

"That mean you started working here when you were seventeen, right?"

"So what?" said Brwa.

Hewa had a point. "So now I can tell. Maybe he did fuck you, too, when you were young," Hewa finally said. "Didn't you say he also was going to fuck a nice boy if he gets one?" Hewa moved from his seat carefully. "How did you get that idea, if you're not one of his victims?"

"Fuck, I told you that was a while ago." Brwa rose from his chair. "I meant you, but you always understand things later. When you didn't reply right away, I knew you didn't know what I was trying to say. But I can understand why—it's because you're still immature," said Brwa.

"Oh, I'm not immature; I know a lot," Hewa said with a smirk.

"What do you know? Let me see. Did you see any? Did you touch them? I don't think so?" Brwa grinned.

"When the time comes, I will see it like everybody else," said Hewa.

"When the time comes?" Brwa repeated sarcastically. "Better say when your cock becomes a rubber, and you dry out." Hewa didn't respond but I laughed at them. "Tell me one thing truly, okay? How many times a day do you use your hand. Don't be shy; we all used to do it, okay?" Brwa said softly.

"Just normal," replied Hewa.

"What's normal?" Brwa chuckled, turning to face me.

"Yeah, he's right; what's normal?" I added.

"God, I mean I don't do it just to have wet dreams; that's it." Hewa grimaced.

"We all do it when we're single; it's as simple as that, but you're shy to tell the truth, right?" said Brwa.

"That's right," I replied instead.

"See, he wasn't afraid to tell the truth, because he isn't shy like you. How many times are you doing it a day?" Brwa ask me.

"I don't count them," I replied finally.

"Uncountable!" said Brwa, chuckling.

"No, that's not what I mean?" I said, laughing.

"A while ago, he said he didn't do it. Now he says he doesn't count them," Brwa continued. "You know what? Before I got married, I had a friend like you. He was still single, and he asked his father to help him get married, but his father was financially short-handed. He was an old man and they were a poor family, but very respectable and nice." Hewa took out his cigarette box and lit one. "When his father got tired of his always asking for help to get married, the old man told him at last, "As far as I can see, you'll never be able to get married until you behave like that. Your ass will be your only wife." I didn't understand that in the beginning, but later I figured it out. Do you know what I'm talking about?" Brwa asked as he continued to enjoy his cigarette, and smoke whirled out from his mouth. "His father meant that he'd have to jerk it off, because he wasn't going to do anything about helping him get married." Brwa threw his cigarette butt on the ground and stamped it with his foot.

It was getting darker and the electric lights on the street went on. "It's a nice night," uttered Brwa. We said nothing. "It's nice now to be home and put all the children to sleep, and in your room, you put the fan on and cover the windows. You turn off the light, undress yourself, and lie down on your back in the bed, and she's sitting on top of you, and after couple hours of lovemaking, you sleep until late morning. When you wake up, you take a nice shower, and she makes breakfast. And after you eat your breakfast, you put your clothes on and come out to your daily routine. That's fun, spending a night like that, and I've had quite few of them. I know you both are dreaming about that day, I'm I right?" asking Brwa.

"Whatever, that's what Rebeen's dreaming of," said Hewa.

"You're itching for it, more than I do," I replied.

"Kak Brwa, you'd better not talk about this topic anymore, because he's going to have wet dreams tonight. We'd better change that subject," Hewa suggested.

"Changing the subject doesn't do any good for his hardened penis to get soft," said Brwa. "I'm sure he'll make his pants wet tonight." They laughed at me.

"You go get some sleep for now. I know we gave you a headache. We were just joking with you," said Hewa. "Don't be upset. You know, the night's too long, and if we don't make some fun, we get bored. But make sure if you want to have a hand job, go use the bathroom. Don't make the sleeping sheets dirty; we're going to use them later," Hewa instructed.

"Shut your mouth," I said, grimacing. "Don't you see? It's night, and sounds float on the air. All the neighbors are sleeping; don't bother them."

I walked in to the small rooms, put my rifle by the bed, and turned off the light. I got in bed, covered myself with a sheet, put my right hand over my eyes, and eventually fell asleep. When I woke up later, I checked my pants. It was normal—my penis was normal. It was about 3:00 AM when I glanced at my wristwatch. I leaped out of bed and took my rifle and went outside until sunrise.

After a Nap

By the time I woke-up, Brwa and Hewa were still sitting outside on the chairs, talking. I got out of bed, relaxing my arms in the air, cracking my backbones, and making a long yawn. I cleaned my nose with a tissue and shook my head few times, trying to shock sleep out from my head. I splashed some water on my face, put on my shoes, took my rifle, and stepped out to the alley through the open door.

"Did you have wet dreams, or did you masturbate before you went to bed?" Hewa asked me. "Can we still use the sheets or did you make it dirty?"

I didn't reply

"He seems satisfied now," said Brwa. "I was watching you in the window, moving your hand between your legs. You moved it rapidly." They laughed at me. "I believe you were cuming on the tile, not the bed. Did you clean the floor already?"

"I guess you are trying to make me quit this job and run away. Stop acting childishly and think about something else. Stop making fun of me," I warned them. I had grown tired of them.

"We have no problem making fun of you" said Hewa, I guess Brwea tricked him to his side while I was slept, but I new that they just want to make me angry and have some fun "We just like driving you crazy"

I keep quite but Hewa went on "Make this long night pass with some fun. If we just sit down without making some jokes, we get bored."

Brwa nodded in agreement.and smilled he put one hand on my shoulder "You better not take it so seriously because that's just a beginning. There are a lot more nights to come, and on each of them, we will find a way to amuse ourselves. But tonight, it started with you; tomorrow, it might be Hewa's turn."

"He's not come back yet?" I asked.

"Who's not come back?" Brwa didn't get it.

"The boss," I explained.

"Why do you care? You're not his wife," said Hewa.

"Fuck you," I said. "You have a big mouth."

Hewa laughed, knowing he was driving me crazy.

"No, he's not back," replied Brwa. "Why? Are you going to tell him we're bothering you?"

"Don't worry; I'm not a little kid," I said. "I just have a question. Where might he be?"

"Hell, how do we know? Maybe he's in a meeting. He didn't tell us where he went or where he goes," explained Brwa.

"Maybe he's spending a night with one of his women friends"," I said.

Brwa shook his head. "I don't think so. He doesn't go after them; they come here on their own."

"They don't have a husband or family? Why don't they have any fear?" I inquired.

"What you talking about it? Don't you see all these whore houses around the city?" said Brwa

"I heard that story as I told you erlier, but Hewa wasn't believed me, we like you tell us what you know about it?"

"Are you a news reporter or what? Why do you investigate those things? As they say, you'd better put your hand over your hat and make sure a wind is not blowing out. You get it?" Brwa asked.

"I don't investigate anything. I'd just like to know how that happened. I won't tell anyone—I promise. I just have to know things, and I don't understand—those girls are still young and have a long future ahead of them. Don't they think that no one will marry them in the future if they lose their virginity?" I explained.

"If they lose their virginity?" Brwa sneered. "They already did. They're not suitable to make a family anymore. Would you marry one of them?"

"Of course not; who would?" I replied. "Do you think I'm an idiot?"

"No one said you are," said Brwa.

"I wish I'd seen them just once to see what they look like," I said. "I'd like to know who they are."

"As I told you, every Thursday afternoon you can come and see them. It's just that simples" Brwa informed me.

"But we're not scheduled to work on Thursday," I said.

"Oh, that's right," said Brwa. "Did you want me to tell them to stop by on Wednesday or Tuesday because Mr. Rebeen wants to meet with them?" Brwa asked. "I work then, so you can come here and say you want to see me or that you left something here that you forgot, like your jacket, for example."

"That's a good Idea; I will do that," I said.

"It's almost five-thirty now. We will leave in two or three more hours at most." Brwa glanced at his watch, yawning. "I'd better go to bed as soon as I reach home. I'm getting blind for some sleep."

Birds started coming out from their nests and chirpings in the trees all over the house gardens. The sun slowly came into view, making the sky clearer. Some people started to appear, going to their workplaces.

Hewa put a teapot on the little gas stove to brew some tea. Brwa lit a cigarette and puffed out the smoke through his nose. I sat on the chair, put my hands behind my head, and relaxed. I closed my eyes for a moment as I yawned. When the tea was ready, each of us drank a cup. Then our friends started appear for the dayshift, one by one.

Brwa, Hewa, and I left for the bus station, rifles on our shoulders. When we got to the station, Brwa said good-bye to us and went to the other side of the street toward the west, where he lived. When the bus arrived, Hewa and I got in and found our spots.

"From now on, I will believe you. You were right about those high school girls," said Hewa. "I wonder who they are. I'd better come with you on Thursday. We can find a reason for being there if they ask."

"It's not a bad idea, and they know we're best friends," I replied.

"I have Brwa's cell phone number. We can call him first, before we go.

I nodded. "We'll do that."

"Remind me tomorrow and I will leave my jacket there, and on Thursday, we can call Brwa, and we can go. Then we'll get a chance to see those fucking whores," said Hewa. "I'm getting crazy for Thursday to come, but we have no choice. We have to be patient until then."

"Don't worry. If you're patient, we will see them and know them just like Brwa. After all, we can't do anything. They don't care about us. They're just going under the special golden penis he has," I said.

"That's exactly right. Ours are not golden like his, even though we're younger," said Hewa.

"You don't get it. He has money he pays them—that's what I mean," I explained. "But what I don't understand is how this son of a bitch finds those little teenage cunts. That's what I'm not able to understand. After all, who's going to marry them? I don't think he was so kind, while they're naked, to have mercy on them. Who can control himself when some little teenage girls—seventeen or eighteen years old—are naked before him?"

"You better seal this subject. I'm almost cuming in my pants on this bus. Let us talk about something else," Hewa requested.

"Okay, we will talk about it tomorrow night when we go back there, not now on this bus. I can't hide it if it's waking." We chuckled.

When the bus reaching its destination, we got out and went to the little grill shop. We has a tow shish of liver lamb with grilled tomatoes and onion. We sat down in the stalls and enjoyed our meal. Afterward, we went to a teahouse close by to drink a couple teas. Hewa lit a cigarette after he drank his tea as he waited for me to finish.

"How many cigarettes do you smoke a day?" I asked him.

"Around six or eight. I am a light smoker."

"You better quit," I suggested. "Doesn't do you any good."

"I'll think about it," replied Hewa. He stamped the filter in the ashtray on the table and rose from his chair. We paid and left there at once, saying good-bye to each other when we reached the corner where we usually departed. Each of us went in a different direction. On the busy streets, city inhabitants all roamed around everywhere, the chaos of selling and buying in the streets mixed with the shouting of sellers to the public for their goods, make that morning atmosphere more alive.

We Discover More Secrets

Around four o'clock that afternoon, I woke up and made a long yawn. I didn't use my alarm clock but always woke up during the usual time every day. I started work around six o'clock in the evening and came home about eight in the morning.

After gathering my thoughts, I remembered that tomorrow I was supposed to go to see those high school girls around two I just like to see them, what if I found one of them who's I knew? Will I doubt it, but anyway I will find out tomorrow. I thought, if I woke up this late tomorrow, I wouldn't be able to make it.

I got out of bed, washed my face in the sink, and went to the kitchen to warm up some food over the gas stove. Then I took a quick shower.

I walked to the bus station around five o'clock, and the bus arrived shortly afterward. I looked around for Hewa but he was not anywhere to be found.

Out side the government official's house, Sardar, Shorrsh, and Brwa were standing with a guy who visited Brwa sometimes. A pickup truck was parked in front of the house.

"Good evening, guys," I greeted my friends.

"Good evening," they replied.

"Welcome to Treasure Island," said Shorrsh who's been a guard with M for few years, he was took off last night.

I shook hands with them.

"Is Hewa here yet?" I inquired.

"No, we haven't see him yet," they replied.

"He will show up at any minute," said Brwa.

"He's never been late except for that day when his mom was sick, and he called in that afternoon. I don't know if she's feeling better now or not," Shorrsh said.

"He's really a nice guy and easy to get along with," said Brwa. "He never takes anything seriously, and even if we make him mad, he forgets it in the next minute."

At the corner of the alley, Hewa appeared. He had his rifle on his shoulder as usual, and he was wearing jeans that he'd bought few days ago. He looked tired.

"We were just talking about you," I greeting him with a smile.

Hewa greeted us and then said, "I'm a little tired. I didn't sleep very well

"What's going on?" I inquired.

"I don't know. A bunch of kids were playing in the alley and screaming all day long. I hardly slept," Hewa explained. "You can't do anything about it—you know kids."

"I will switch shifts with you," I offered. "Whenever you feel like you need a rest, just go ahead and sleep as much as you want."

"Yeah, maybe that'll work," Hewa agreed.

"I slept good today. I'm alone at home, and not many kids live in that area to bother me," I explained.

"I appreciate it; let's see how it works," said Hewa.

"It's the same routine for us today," said Shorrsh. "Work and home, home and work, repeatedly spending our lives without knowing where we are heading. What else can we do in the winter?"

"If it was a spring maybe we could go out to the mountain for a picnic during our day off, but we have to wait for months to get there," said the guy who visits Brwa sometimes.

Hewa disagreed. "I'm not really interested in a picnic. People go to the mountain, and get drunk, and eat all day long, and dance and sing. We have a lot more important things in life to worry about, but I guess no one really cares. It's stupid when you have too many other important issues in life but put all your attention only on singing and dancing. To me, it's nonsense."

"That's all we have left," said Brwa. "You said too many important issues, but you better say too much pressure. No one knows what will become of us. Everyone tries to get as much as they can get in life. Most of us are without a point or goal; we're just waiting for death. That's a disaster to me." When we didn't respond, he went on. "The epidemic of dishonesty, always fighting over money, that's faced this community of ours for so many years makes most of us sick and desperate. We're just hovering in the same circle and we have the same problems repeatedly—for example, no gas, no electricity, no housing—and every day, prices keep going up and up. People complain without any result from the government, and those in charge, as we can see from this official"—Brwa pointed toward the house—"live their lives as they want. After all, we're also part of this injustice, no matter if we like it or not. We protect them with our bodies and souls. We have to blame ourselves first, because we believe in their lies, their fake promises. Our government blames other countries to explain their shortcomings, until no one complains anymore." Brwa sat down on the chair, took another cigarette, and lit it. "We make ourselves happy when they appear on TV, telling us a bunch of lies. They know how to play their cards with folks' minds and collect wealth, get houses, companies in Europe, or even in the country. Nowadays, everywhere you go is occupied by those tyrants."

"I'm not with you on that point," said Awat, who have been listning to them behind the wall, inside the house, when he emerged they all got upset to his action "Because while they are in the mountains, they put their chests in front of bullets every day to free this country. Most of us in this city were not able to argue with dictators before the revolution so why blame them if they get a house or wealth today? Don't you deserve your salary at the end of the month while you're here always on time according to your schedule?" Awat continued. "After all, they didn't do it for themselves; they did it to help us survive the dictators. How many of our mothers, daughters, and sisters have been in prison for years, and they have been raped and got pregnant? How much women's underwear and bras was found in the day of revolution in dictator's prisons? We shouldn't forget all that," Awat complained.

"Yes, you are right. I'm with you on that point," said Brwa.

Hewa who have been listened all the while, he interrupted"But remember, they aren't able to do that without folks' support in the city. That day, people from everywhere around the country voluntarily came out from their homes and shared their lives for success in this process. Look back the history around the world—no revolution took place without people's help and support," Hewa said.

Brwa rose from his chair then he said "After all, what's the difference between a dictator and our government, if they are alike in most aspects? As we said, the dictators' men raped our family members in their prisons, but now the members of our government are repeating the same thing in different forms, different ways—not only raping them but occupying their minds as well, leading them to the wrong path. Sometimes, when a poor woman goes out to get a job in some government buildings, they don't hire her if she's not a nice-looking woman. And when they do hire her, gradually the manager gets close to her until, by some tricks, he starts to fool around with her every day in his office. He does whatever he likes to do with her. Is that what we call freedom?" Brwa asked.

"I know, but that's not everyone or everywhere," I interrupted. "It depends on the type of person. You can't say that everyone working in the government building behaves like that. No one can push the women to do anything if they're not up to it. Besides, those women we are talking about here are always like that, no matter where they work or live. Some of them even use their houses for that purpose. Some of them are housewives. For example, we know those high school girls visit this house. They're not working in the government offices, and they all teenagers not mature. Who brought them here? or how did they come up to this? Are they looking for jobs? No, but they're teenagers, you can change their mind with few sweet words, or promises. However we don't know for sure, how they involved, besides who's tricked them, but at lest I feel that their families unaware of what they do, or where they go after school, but these are all guesses, it could be right, it could be not"

"I have no doubt that M use some tricks to make the girls come to this, but we all know that sixteen-, seventeen-, or eighteen-year-olds easily believe men," said Awat, "especially someone in the high-ranking positions like our boss. Maybe he promised the first one that he'd marry her. We all know that the dream of girls that age is to find a soul mate, a rich man, a leader, someone famous and well known. Age doesn't matter, but the problem is that women in our country just look for someone rich. It doesn't matter how he got rich or how old he is," complained Awat. "Those girls we talk about come here weekly and sleep with this monkey. This monkey also has a girl at the university in Europe—it's literally just like they sleep with their dad, or he sleeps with his daughters. May I be a sacrifice for you, Lord. Why did you give them all that?" said Awat, facing to heaven. "Who knows? Maybe his daughter in Europe sleeps with a different guy every day. As they say, what goes around, comes around. They're young and don't know what's going to happen in their future by doing this. They don't know he's just doing this for his own pleasure, but I'm sure the first girl he slept with was one that one of his customers brought for him. I mean, those women we see sometimes have found girls for him. Maybe that first girl was one of the daughters of those whores the official slept with some nights. Who knows? As they say, elders splash water and the young plays in it. See what I mean? They are learning what their mother do."

"You're a smart man; you're like a fiction narrator," I said. "You just make the story, so what are you doing here, wasting your time working with us? You have a talent. Why don't you go write all these stories and publish them. You can make good money; I'm not kidding," I advised Awat.

"Did you think that's funny? I'm serious; those things come as a net, and whores, wherever they are, find each other and work together. It's like a business, and the men who are after them most likely don't stay with a woman. They use that one to pull more. As I said, those prostitutes know each other very well. They find men for one another, and you can recognizing them just by looking in their eyes," Awat said.

A taxi appeared and stopped in front of us. Aras was got out from the taxi, and he had his rifle in his hand. "How's your night going, guys?" he asked when he got out.

"Going dark," I replied sarcastically.

"We're chatting here and waiting for someone to resolve that mystery," said Hewa.

"Maybe you could," I said.

"What kind of mystery?" Aras inquired. "If it's a political mystery, I have no clue, but if it's about war, maybe I can help."

"No, it's something far more than what you thought, and I believe you know something about it. It's up to you if you want to fix that puzzle, or maybe you just have as much as information we have, but I guess you have more. I can see it in your eyes," Hewa said.

"What are you talking about?" said Aras.

"We're talk about the net here," said Hewa.

"You mean Internet or phone?" Aras inquired.

We giggled. "No, that's not what we meant," said Hewa.

"So what is it then?" Aras asked suspiciously.

"We're trying to understand the mystery of this house—and those high school girls," Hewa said clearly.

"What high school girls?" Aras inquired.

"Don't confuse us more than we already are. You know what I'm I talking about. We all know it, but we think you have more information than we do," Hewa informed him.

"What makes you believe that I have more information than you do?" Aras inquired.

"Because you're around during the day most of the time," Hewa explained. "And we're not."

"Oh, you mean those girls who come here on Thursday afternoons and the boss teaches them a lesson inside and out?" Aras said finally.

"See? First you ask 'what high school girls?' Now you say he's teaching them a lesson inside and out. What do you mean, inside and out?" asked Hewa.

"I mean boss teaches them inside the house and how to satisfy him in all positions. After that, he also teaches them how to hunt the other baby deer like themselves out there and present them to him here," Aras explained. "He's a devil; he knows how to hunt those gals and feed them a white milk, until they grow up and become harsh whores like their mothers."

"Are they all into this with their moms also?" I inquired.

"No, not all of them, but the first one whose virginity he took was a daughter of one of his customers. Her mom sent her over. The mother was beautiful, until one day he asked her to bring her daughter over. The daughter was much more beautiful than the mom, and he couldn't let her escape from his dirty hand. He just gave them money and pricked her little cunt off. It wasn't long before her friends enjoyed the net," Aras explained.

"But how could her mother be so stupid to do that with her own daughter? Is she an idiot?" Hewa asked.

"You can say that. If she wasn't idiot, why would she cheat on her husband? I will tell you what was going on, but keep it to yourself, okay?" Aras got closer. He grabbed a chair and we sat all around him in a circle. "One day, about six months ago, this whore came here," Aras began. "I was in front of the door, outside the house, sitting on the chair, like now. I was checking my text message on my cell phone." Aras scratched the back of his neck with fingertip. "Anyway, she came in front of me suddenly, and I looked at her face. First, I thought she might be asking for some address, but she's wanted to see the boss. That was the first time I saw her." He hesitated for a moment and then continued. "She asked me if he was home, and I gave some thought before I replied. I said that he was home, and she stepped inside without my permission." Aras buried his hand in his pocket, took out his badge and clip it on his shirt pocket, than he went on"I told her, 'Excuse me, you can't just walk in like that.' I told her to tell me who she was and what she wanted. I was mad when she behaved like that, just like I'm a kid playing in front of the house. She didn't pay any attention to me; she acted like someone who just came back from the bar, late at night. She was putting on very nice makeup, and her lips were so red, shining in the sunlight like pomegranate seeds. Also, she had a black dot over her upper lip.

"She was around thirty-five, I guess. Her fragrance smelled so strong that it jammed my brain right away. She had a very sexy figure, and as she talked to me, she swayed her hips. Her hips were full in her long beige skirt, and she was rolling the sleeves of her black shirt. She had a few gold bracelets around her wrist. Her black, almond-shaped eyes were shining with mascara. The back of her black shirt was so thin that I could see the line of her bra in the back. She finally asked me to tell him that she was here, and I asked, 'Who should I say is here?' She smiled and said, 'Just tell him there is a woman who wants to see him, the one he talked to last night on the phone.' I went in and told the boss about her and that she wouldn't give her name. He was wearing a pair of pajamas and was watching TV. He got up and went to the window, where he could see her in the garden, bending over to smell the roses. When he saw her, he told me to let her in. When I showed her to his door, he was still wearing pajamas. "He told me then that if anyone came to see him, I should tell that person that he was not there, and if his son came, I should say he was sleeping.

"After the two of them spent a couple good hours inside, she came out walked past me as I sat on my chair under the shade of the tree. She didn't even say good-bye or anything, but her hair was messed up, she was brushing it with her hand. She was sniffing the palms of her hands, walking faster than usual, until she disappeared into the alley at the corner. Just before she did, she looked back with a smile on her face."

"But what does this have to do with those high school girls?" I interrupted.

"You will see; be patient," Aras continued. "One day, about four weeks later, she came back, but this time she had a green purse over her shoulder and a bunch of keys in her hand. Her fingernails were polished a pink color, and she had light makeup on. This time when she saw me, she smiled and asked, 'Is he home now?' It was as if she was teasing me—she knew he was home. Then she walked right in, as if to say it was her house now. This time, though, when she went in, she didn't close the hallway door. After a while, I looked through the window to see if they were in the living room, but they were not. I slowly went in and walked toward the kitchen—I thought if they saw me, I'd say I wanted to fill the water bucket, as it was a hot summer day in the middle of August. Anyway, the door of his bedroom was closed, but I heard them talking." Aras put his hand between his legs, smiling. "Guys, I get horny whenever I remember the situation. I got a little closer to the door and listened to them—they were discussing a high school girl, and M asked, 'Is she beautiful?' And the woman said, 'Yeah, more beautiful than myself, and she's sweet.' Then they kissed—I could tell because the sound of humming was loud and clear as they sucked each other's mouths. I knew he was inside her.

"Does she know about our relationship?' M inquired. And she responded, 'Yeah, she does. We have a lot in common.' Then M asked if the girl was experienced, and the woman said that no, she was still too young for that. That's when M suggested that she bring the girl over sometime. The woman asked, 'Why? Are you going to do her too?' And M said, 'Only if you both agree.' The woman said, 'But I don't want you to take her virginity. She's still young for that.' M asked if the girl had a nice body, and when the woman said yes, she did, M said, 'I will just try to do her in the back door; I promise."

"The woman told M to be patient until next time, that she had to think about it and discuss it with the girl. 'I don't want to force her if she's chooses not to,' she said. M agreed with that, and the woman then said, 'Let's go through the back door.'

"I was frightened when I heard that—I thought they would come out from another door and catch me there. Quickly, I went back to the kitchen and waited for few minutes, but they didn't came out. Later, I figured out that she meant to do her in the back door. Carefully, I got close to the room once again and listened to them. I heard her—'Oh, yeah, oh'— in pleasure, as you see in the porn movies. I looked through the keyhole. M was slapping her hips and pumping her hard. I was afraid at that moment that someone might see me, but no one came, and when he was about to cum, he took it out, and she straightened her body on the bed, and he put it in her mouth. I was hard like a rock, so I slowly backed off and went out, outside to the living room. I put my shoes on and went to our bathroom in the corridor and started masturbating until I cum and got relieved. After that, I imagined her in my mind whenever I had sex with my wife. I went back to my chair and tried not to think about what I saw. When she finally came out and left, she walked through the alleyway, and I can tell you, she wasn't walking normally. I saw that she threw something she taken from her purse, so later, I searched the ground, right where she was dropped the thing, and I found it—it was a condom."

How I Got Here

"I am not sure how that came to my mind, when one day I told Shorrsh that I was out of work," said Aras.while we're gathered in front of M's house that night "He told me that he would like to find a job for me if I would accept the offer. I didn't know what he was doing at the time, because I hadn't seen him for months. It was wintertime then, and I used to work temporary jobs, wherever I could find a job. Mostly, I worked construction, but during the wintertime, work slowed down. I was wandering around from one teahouse to other, gathering with a few friends of mine. That way I took care of myself for short periods of time, just like a bird—I worked in summer and relaxed in winter, but whenever I ran out of work, my pockets were emptied for weeks or months. Sometimes, I didn't even get enough jobs in summer. Then Shorrsh told me that he had been working for this official for four years. At the time, I guess the boss had only one driver with a few guards, and he was asking them to find some friends they trusted and he would hire them. Back then, four years ago, they were paid well. It was much better than house construction, so I accepted the offer—I thought I'd like to work with Shorrsh. I told him I didn't have a rifle, but finally I borrowed some money and bought one," Aras explained.

"You've worked here for four years now? What about Shorrsh?" I interrupted.

"He's been here for eight years, I guess," Aras went on. "I know sometimes those officials drink with their friends, but only on some occasions, once or twice a year. I heard that someone brings them women, and they drink and have fun all night long, especially on holidays." Aras put his hand in his pocket and took out a box of cigarettes. "Every year, his wife comes back from Europe and spends months here, but somehow, when his wife isn't here and he is alone, they bring some whores and spend a night of pleasure. But that wasn't every week or an everyday routine. Lately, I don't even know how usual it is for him."

"Does his wife know that?" I inquired.

"I don't really know," Aras continued. "But he doesn't listen to his wife. He will get married to a younger gal if his wife says something that bothers him. As they say, when a man gets rich, he will kill a man or get a new wife. Someone like our boss will do both of them, if he wishes. Anyway, one day, my wife's uncle asked me to help him move furniture for the new house he had just rented." Aras took a cigarette from the box and lit it. "So I took off few hours that day to help him. When I get here, Shorrsh was in the room watching TV, and later we talked about kids. He has a son in elementary school and school just opened for few weeks before this time. That reminded him that a girl had come here, wearing a school uniform and asking for our boss. She only would say that she wanted to see him, but she wouldn't give her name. She just said, 'Tell him Awaz's daughter wants to see him.'

"When Shorrsh told me that, I knew that Awaz was the woman who had come the other day. The girl went in, after the boss gave permission, and she came out shortly afterward and left without word," Aras informed us. "When I mentioned this incident to Shorrsh, he told me what he'd seen and heard the other day. I didn't believe him at first, but about a week later, that girl showed up again. And she arrived with her friend—they both were dressed in school uniforms, and after that, we saw them with their school bags hanging from their shoulders—that was the day when Hewa came to start his first day of work. So she and the other girl go in, and after about a half-hour, her friend came out and left, but the first girl remained inside. Probably two or three hours later, she finally left. It was dark and she seemed so confused, we weren't sure what had happened inside, but we guessed the boss did her inside that afternoon. The next day, when the garbage truck came to the alley, we emptied all the garbage cans in the house, and I found a few pieces of white cloth, reddened with blood, in his room's wastebasket. Then we understood that we'd been right about what we thought." Aras finished the story and lit other cigarette.

"Motherfucker M, he have no fear?," I said.

"Of course not, and why he would be afraid, if her mom send her over?" Aras inquired

"Did you meant she's Awaz's daughter? I'm right?" I inquired

"Right, I meant her daughter" replied Aras

""But can M take the girls virginity, even if he have permission from her mom?" I said "Is he think about consciences in the future?"

"What did you mean?" Aras inquired

"I mean this girl will not get marriage in the future?" I explained

"So?" said Aras

"But who's going to get marriage with her in this condition?' I explained "We're not live in Europe or west"

"Don't worry she don't need marriage, maybe that's what her mother give birth for" said Aras "Who knows maybe she's from some other man, not Awaz's husband"

"Could be, everything possible from a woman like Awaz" I said

" Let me ask you something." Aras folded his hand on his chest. "Let's say she never sent her daughter for him, but she slept with him behind her husband's back, if she has one. When a man want to gets married, there are questions about the family background. Whoever want to get marriage with a girl, will ask like everybody else does. When the man whoever he's, finds out her mother is a whore, do you think this man will marry her?" Aras explained.

"I don't think so," I replied.

"Would you marry someone like that?" Aras inquired.

"Of course not," I replied.

"So that's going to be her future, too, like her mom, and maybe it's better for her to train her from now on," Aras explained.

"I guess so," I said. "But that's horrible. I don't understand those types of people. How do they see life? Sex is not everything. This world of ours has a lot more to it than you've seen through a keyhole."

"Our boss wants her cunt; that's all he looking for," Aras chuckled. "Besides, they offer him what he wants."

"I am afraid that if one day, our boss doesn't get any of them and he's in the mood, he'll call one of us in and say, take it off. What we should do then?" I asked.

"I don't know; you better run," Aras suggested with smile.

"What a day we're in. That's a same thing with the previous regime, but our government officials practice it in a different way and different forms," I said.

"I guess we cannot make any changes; after all, when your thing gets hard, you have to do something about it. We masturbate and relax our minds, but our boss finds a hole to slip it into," said Aras.

"But you have a wife. Why do you masturbate?" I inquired.

"I mean you, not myself. I used to, when I was in your age and single," Aras explained.

"Is she the only one with whom the boss does it? Or is he doing her friend, too?" I inquired.

"Who knows? He doesn't tell us what he does to them; we just guess. If he didn't do her friend that day, he will do her some other time," Aras replied.

"Maybe he will tape them. He has a camcorder at home," I said.

"Maybe so; why not?" Aras shrugged. "They do whatever they like. That's why they close their eyes to all those whores' business in this country. They eat and fuck and steal folks' wealth and kill whoever they want," said Aras.

"We better shut our mouths and be careful, before we get fucked and killed. As they say, if your tongue lets you, your brain is in rest. That's so true," I said.

"I really hate this life. Whenever I look at myself in the mirror, I think I'm a guard of a whorehouse, not a government official," said Aras. "I'm thinking about getting another job and getting away from this place."

"Yeah, that's what I think, too. Maybe people say we're all doing the same thing here; that's why we shut our mouths," said Hewa, as he turned to leave.

"Of course, if you see the crime and say nothing, you're also counted as a part of it, but can we do anything at all? He's in government. He has power. We'll be killed if we talk about in the public. So the only way is to leave this place as soon as we can and find something else to do," said Aras.

I sighed. "When I hear the news and see all those irresponsible leaders around us, ruling our country, my heart and mind is burdened and melancholy," I said.

Aras took a cigarette from his pocket and offered it to me. He gave me a light with his lighter. I puffed out the smoke and coughed slightly.

"Why do you care, brother?" Aras inquired. "We can't make any difference in others' lives when they chose to live that way. None of those people has anything to do with our lives. People follow their hearts and what makes them comfortable, without thinking of their future. We know that when we die, each of us will go to his own grave, and the Lord take account with us individually. You better not tire your mind with something you have no power over. Everybody knows what's right and what's wrong," explained Aras.

"Yeah, you're right," I agreed. "I better see where Hewa went. Excuse me; I will be back."

I went inside the house and found Hewa in the guards room, watching TV and drinking a cup of tea. He offered me some tea, so I grabbed a tea glass and poured some sugar in the glass; then poured some tea from the kettle.

"Did you see your sweetheart today," Hewa asked conversationally.

"Oh, no, I haven't seeing her since that day," I said. "I don't know where her school is. Besides, I haven't had a chance because I have to sleep until afternoon every day. That makes it hard for me to see her," I explained.

"But you know where she lives, right?" Hewa inquired.

"Yeah, I know, but I haven't had a chance to see her," I replied.

"You can take a day off this week. I'll take a day off, too, and we can spend the night together at your house. Then, first thing in the morning, we can go out and find where she goes to school. What did you think?"

"It's not a bad idea," I agreed. "I'm ready whenever you are."

"Okay, then, how about this Wednesday?" Hewa proposed.

"That's fine with me," I replied.

I finished my tea and washed my tea glass. "Aren't you going to get some sleep?" I asked Hewa.

"I'm going to take a nap now for a couple hours. Wake me whenever you need me," said Hewa.

"I will; don't worry."

Hewa got in the bed and covered himself with a sheet. I switched off the TV and the light, and then went out to sit next to Aras. We chatted until sunrise.

The Day I Talked to My Girlfriend

Today I truly wanted to see those gals that boss has been seducing. I thought that maybe, that way, I would not be tricked by any girls who seemed innocent when you saw them on their way to school, and then you'd find out who they really are. On the other hand, I was thinking about my sweetheart. I haven't talked to her for a while, she might be think that I forgot about her, but I don't blame her at all, my scheudle totally opposite of hers, she go to school during a day, an I working graveyard, so I have to sleep after sunrise, I have no choice, by the time she goes home, I'm still in bed sometimes.

I start thinking about what Aras told us last night. The daughter that whore Awaz, she was the one who slept with M, she had sexual intercourse with him, beside her mom, and Aras said that was about six monthes ago, that Awaz came to M's house for the first time. If I wasn't misunderstood, M lost Awaz's daughter virginty that day, when she came accompanied with afriend, because the gurds found a piece of white cloth soaked in blood, I was wondering if Awaz aware of that!? Everythings possible espicially when we just guessing all this, maby she just find girls for M at school? Who knows?

I ate my lunch and looked through a few books I had on my bookshelf. After a while, I decided to call Hewa. As I waited for him to answer, I roamed around the living room, looking at the walls and checking the corners of the room for no apparent reason. Hewa didn't answer my call, so I hung up and changed my clothes to get ready for work.

"Tomorrow is Wednesday; we're suppose to take a day off,," I murmured as I dressed. When I was ready, I left the house, locked the door, and walked down the alley. I hadn't gone very far when my cell phone start ringing—it was Hewa. He said he'd awakened late, but he now was ready and waiting for me. When I reach his home, he was standing in front of his house.

After we shook hands in greeting, Hewa said, "The first thing we should do is get permission for a day off tomorrow. And I have a plan: I will ask the guards leader in the morning, so no one will think we have a something to do together. I'll let them know that my mom wasn't feeling well last night and that I have to take her to the doctor."

"Good idea," I agreed.

"Where should we go now?" asked Hewa.

"To see Yar" I said which is mean girlfriend in our language "to her school where else did you expect?","

"So, you going to talk to her?" Hewa inquired.

"You will see," I said.

"I mean, are you ready to tell her?" Hewa inquired.

"Yeah, I will, if she gives me a chance," I said.

"But don't you saids we're going tomorrow morning!?," Hewa reminded me.

"If I can see her, I will talk to her today, so we don't have to go tomorrow" I assured him. "But if she doesn't have time or she's with a few of her friends, she might not want to talk to me. After all, you know what people are saying."

"Nowadays, girls are not afraid anymore. Do you forget what's going on at the boss's house? They're all high school girls like her," said Hewa.

"Don't ever say that in my presence, okay?" I grimaced. "She's not a whore; she's from a very respectful family. You will see her in a short while, and you can judge for yourself how she behaves. You can tell if she's a bad person or not."

"I didn't mean to say that. Don't get mad. I just want to see if you are brave enough to talk to her," said Hewa. Then he tap me on the shoulder and fifteen minutes later, we got there.

"Okay, we're close now," I said. "See? Pupils are coming out from her school"

"How did you know she's attending this school?" Hewa inquired

"I'm not sure hundred percent, but she live in this area, and that's only high school around here, so should be it" I explained

"What if you are wrong?"

"Will, let us find out?" I said "Pupils just start came out now, we will look around until I find her"

"If you don't find her today, I'm not coming with you next time" said Hewa

"Let me pay attention to them, I want to know if she's here" I said

"There she is," said Hewa.

I looked in that direction. "You don't know her; don't make me crazy," I said, and Hewa chuckled.

"You're already confused. How are you going to talk to her like that? You are shaking, man. What's all that about?"

"I said shut up now. Don't go any further," I insisted. "Please don't make me lose my chance," I said as she came into view at the corner. "Oh, there she is. No more jokes."

"Which one?" Hewa inquired.

"The one with the blue dress and brown backpack on her shoulder."

"Man, she's gorgeous. Go ahead and talk to her. She's only with her friend," said Hewa. "Just the two of them. You can do that."

"I will; don't worry," I replied quickly. When we got closer to her, I looked at her with a smile on my face. She still hadn't noticed me because she was intent on speaking with her friend. When she finally saw me, she was so exited and surprised.

"Hi! How are you? And where have you been?" Talar said, with a beautiful smile, she's surprised seeing me

.

"I'm fine," I said. "I found a job. I'm working now with a friend of mine." I managed to keep talking, even though there was no doubt that I was shaking, as Hewa told me earlier.

"You're not going back to school?" Talar inquired.

"No, I thought I'd already told you that."

"So, what are you doing now?" Talar asked. "I thought you just came back from school."

"I came out with my friend, and we are supposed to start work around six. I work from six in the evening to six in the morning—the graveyard shift."

"Oh, that's why you're not around. You must sleep during the day," said Talar. "Yeah, you got that right, and here I am," I said. "So how are you doing with school?"

"Doing well, thanks," Talar replied, "So you're a guard with your friend?"

"That's right," I replied. "Are you mad at me?"

"That was him, that guy? The one who sent you a letter?" Talar inquired, instead of answering my question.

"Yes, that's him," I replied. "Is there any chance we can talk sometime?"

"About what?"

"About us—our relationship. We should understand each other more closely. I mean, talking about our future and making a plan, don't you think?"

"Well, we should," Talar agreed. "But this is the only way we can talk, on the way to school—unless you have a better option."

"Honey, there's another way we can try, if you like," I offered. "I can give you my cell phone number. Then you can call me whenever you have a chance. We will talk more on the phone that way, and it's safer for you, too. We can discuss our plans for the future. What do you think?" I asked.

"That's okay," Talar agreed. "It's very sweet of you to call me that."

"Oh, you're sweeter than honey; trust me," I said.

She looked in my eyes and smiled but said nothing. Then I gave her my cell phone number and she took out a pen from her backpack to write it down.

"You can call me during the night, whenever you have chance. I'm up all night long," I informed her. "Do you need anything?"

"No, thanks, I'm fine," Talar replied quickly.

"I love you," I said.

"Yeah, I love you, too," Talar said, smiling.

"I'll wait to hear from you, and good-bye for now," I finally said.

Hewa walking slowly ahead of me in the alley until I finished talking with Talar. I moved fast to catch with him, and when I was walking alongside him, Hewa asked, "What did she said?"

"She asked if I'm going back to school, and I said no."

"Does she want you to go back to school?" Hewa asked.

"Yeah, that's what she has told me from the first day we met."

"Then what did she said?" Hewa inquired.

"She said she loves me," I replied. "I call her honey, and she was so excited when I said that. And I gave her my cell phone number. I told her to call me any time she wants, and she said she will."

We walked through the alleys toward the main street and passed by some other schools. Pupils came out from their schools, ready to go home. I was very happy.

"Now we're going to find out who those girls are that our boss seduces," I said.

We ran hastily to catch the bus, and we jumped on just as it was pulling away. We hurried to take our seats and paid the guy who was collecting money from the passengers.

This time, as we got close to the house, we looked around for high school girls, but there was no trace of any. When we reached the house, one of the guards, Awat, came out to greet us with a smile. "What are you guys doing here? I thought you were off today."

"No, we're taking tomorrow off," said Hewa.

Awat nodded. "So what do you guys have planned for tomorrow?"

"Just taking some rest, nothing else," replied Hewa.

"Did you take your mom to the doctor today?" Awat asked Hewa.

"My brother took her to the doctor; she's little better now. Thank you for asking," Hewa said.

"So do you guys have any special plan for today?" Awat inquired.

"Not really. We're always together, even though we're not working, that's how we've always been," replied Hewa.

"God keep your friendship and be brothers always," Awat praised us. "So how's the product of farmers this year? You guys have a farm in your village, right?"

"It's not bad," I said, "but not too good either. The last few years there was a drought. Most of the farmers didn't get much product. And people everywhere praying for rain."

"But how does God let the rain drop down from the sky when people behave like our boss?" asked Awat. "It's from God's mercy that he doesn't rain stones upon us. Whenever I think about this lustful dog that I'm guarding, I almost go out of my skin."

"Have the girls showed up today?" Hewa inquired.

"No, they never come on Wednesday," Awat explained. "Is that why you're here?"

"No, we forgot a book yesterday," Hewa insisted. "I know they show up on Thursday, but when you talked about them, I thought they showed up today

"No, they didn't, but you know he also gets women whenever he wants. One phone call—that's all it takes to find his penis buried in a warm vagina."

"Yeah, we all know that," Hewa agreed.

"It should be clear what is it!?"

"We'd better be going before sunset to spend sometime in the teahouse," said Hewa.

"Okay, guys, enjoy your time. I'm not going to be here Thursday, but you still can come. As I told you, around two or two-thirty is the best time to see them," said Awat.

We went back to the street and waited there until the bus arrived. We took a bus to the city center, and in the market we went to the teahouse. After we finished our tea, we took the bus home.

We Take a Day Off

Hewa opened the refrigerator door in the guards room, looking for tomatoes, but he couldn't find any. He shut the door and went out to ask the other guards, "Guys, are the tomatoes all gone?"

"I guess the day-shift guards used them for lunch. You can go to that shop on the corner to buy some," replied Dyari. one of the guards

"Are you hungry already?" I asked Hewa.

"Yeah, I am. You're not hungry?" Hewa inquired.

"Little bit, but I will eat later," I replied.

"Can you buy some tomatoes in the shop on the corner for me?" Hewa asked. "Buy two kilos, please. I will pay you back,"

I went to the shop, walking from the dark alley with a flashlight in my hand and my rifle over my shoulder. I bought two kilos of tomatoes, as Hewa told me, and also some oranges. When I got back, Hewa was in the guards room, peeling onions, while tears dropped from his eyes.

"Who are you crying for?" I teased him.

"Did you come back?" said Hewa. "Can you please wash them off on the sink?"

"I will, and you better go wash your hands and face if you're finished," I suggested.

Hewa put the knife down on the plate and went to the sink, washing his hands and face with soap and drying them with a towel. Then he went out to the corridor to get some air. I started washing a few tomatoes over the sink and put them on the table for him. Later, Hewa cut them and then mixed them with onions. He put some vegetable oil in the pan and heated it over the gas stove. When it was hot, he dumped the mixed tomatoes and onion in the pan. A drop of hot oil spattered on his hand. "Oh, my God! That's hot!" Hewa shouted, hopping around in pain.

He shook his hand and ran to the sink and opened the faucet of cold water over his hand. The spot of the hot oil was visible on his hand, and it looked sore. He opened the refrigerator and took a cup of ice from the freezer. He crushed the ice with a little hammer and then applied it to the burned spot on his hand. I tried to fry tomatoes for him, picking up from where he'd left off, and then I added some salt into it.

"Can you take out three eggs, mix them, and pour it over the tomatoes, please?" Hewa asked me.

"Yeah, I will," I replied. "How do you feel?"

"It's really sore," Hewa sighed.

I mixed the eggs with the tomatoes and onion for him, and when it was ready, I extinguished the fire and brought the pan to the small table in the middle of the room. I put some nan in the bread basket and placed it on the little tray. Then I took out the plastic container of water from the refrigerator and with two glasses, and I filled the glasses with water. We cut a slice of bread and enjoyed our dinner.

"I'm starving," said Hewa as he ate.

"I'm not that hungry. When I talk to my sweetheart, automatically, I'm full. I forget everything right away, even myself. Her speech makes me full of energy."

"I guess if she talks to you every day a few times, you'll quit eating!" Hewa teased.

"Man, you don't know what it's like. Find one and you will see. Love someone and be loved—it's like you're flying in heaven," I explained excitedly.

"Flying in the heaven?" Hewa repeated. "What's the city look like when you're up there? And when do you land?"

I ignored his jesting and asked, "Did you ask for permission for tomorrow?"

"Not yet. You ask first. You have to ask the leader," said Hewa. "You know him?"

"Yeah, I know him. I will ask as soon as we finish," I replied.

"So what are we going to do tomorrow? Did you have anything in mind?" Hewa asked.

"I haven't been in the parks since I left the city. If you like, we could go to some parks," I suggested.

"Don't forget that you will come to my house for tomorrow night; you're invited," Hewa said. "Also tomorrow, while we're both having our day off, we will come back to see those gals. I brought a book with me so I can leave it here as an excuse to come back for it on Thursday."

"It's a good idea," I said, "but I didn't see any book with you when we came."

Hewa took a book from the pocket of his baggy pants. The title on the book was *The Black Flower: Six Short Stories*. "Did you read this?" Hewa asked me.

"No, did you?"

"Yes, I did. You should read it. The first story is about love between rich girls and poor boys. It's all about wealthy people and poor people. When they fall in love, their relationships won't survive. All of them are heartbreaking stories. They're good lessons for someone like you." Hewa handed the book to me.

I opened it and read a few paragraphs from the first page, then leafed through the pages. "That's a nice story; I can tell," I said. "Can I borrow it?"

"Sure, but for now, we going to leave it here. When we come back on Thursday, then you can have it."

Hewa went out from the guards room, and I washed the pan and spoons. When I finished, I went out to join him, and saw that Dyari and Brwa were standing outside the house, chatting with Hewa.

"Is Rebeen inside?" I heard Dyari ask as I came out.

"So, you don't have any days off, like us?" I asked Brwa.

"Oh, yeah, but I'm covering for Shorrsh tonight," Brwa explained.

"Nice to have you here with us," I said.

Later that night, I came out from the guards room, looking for Hewa, and I spotted his shadow—he was standing with Brwa under the light in the alley. I signaled to him to come inside, and I put my index finger over my mouth to let him know to be silent.

"Have you seen my lighter?" Hewa asked in a normal tone.

"Yah, I have it," I replied as I walked toward him.

When I got closer, Hewa asked in a low voice, "What's this all about?"

"Follow me," I whispered. We walked toward a window of the boss's bedroom, which was located in the back of the house by the garbage cans. Through a gap in the curtain, I showed Hewa what I'd seen earlier—red women's lingerie, laying on his bed.

"How did you discover that?" Hewa asked, .

"I just came to dump the garbage," I informed him. "I looked through the curtain's gap and saw that on the bed." Next to the red lingerie was a little plastic bag, the size of a matchbox. "His wife is not here. What's it doing on his bed?"

We decided to see if his room was locked—he always locked it when he left, but we wondered if maybe this time, he'd forgotten to lock it. We went inside to the kitchen and turned the TV on. We peeped out the window to see if anyone was around, and then, carefully, I headed to the room, moving the doorknob until it clicked open. "I told you we should try!" I said to Hewa.

We went in and found the women's red lingerie and the little plastic bag—it turned out to be a condom box. We also discovered a girl's white underwear on the floor under the bed frame. I bent down and picked it up carefully by the edge, hanging it in front of me. The front part of it was covered in dry semen. I held it for Hewa to see.

"Look at this," I said, chuckling.

"Man, put it down. Let's go before they find us in here," said Hewa, grabbing my hand.

"Don't be scared. He's not coming back now," I said.

"We're going to lose our jobs if they find us here," Hewa warned me.

"You better check out from the window," I suggested.

Hewa went back to the kitchen and looked out the window. Nothing had changed. He turned the TV volume to a lower position and came back to the room quickly. I put my head under the bed frame.

"What the hell are you doing there?" Hewa whispered.

I moved back out from under the bed, and in my hand I held two more pieces of underwear, one black and one pink; both of them smelled of old urine. Hewa frowned. "Fuck, he gave them a shower of pee," I said, and Hewa chuckled.

"Put it away, son of a heaven," said Hewa. "Let's get out of here."

I put the underwear back under the bed and scanned the room one more time, savoring my search for another minute. Finally, we went out and closed the door behind us. At the kitchen sink, I washed my hands and then went to the guards room, where Hewa was waiting for me.

"Now, we can say we have evidence," said Hewa.

"Now we can say we live in a whorehouse," I said listlessly.

"Without our fucking one," said Hewa amiably.

"We're not calling ourselves pimps, either," I said.

"No, we're not; we're serving our country," said Hewa. "We're good servants for our beloved hero man."

"At least we're not here on Thursday afternoons when this is going on around here," I said.

"Should we come tomorrow to see those gals?" Hewa inquired. "Are you still interesting to see them?"?"

"Yah, we will come tomorrow, but not because I interesting to see them, but because I like to know who they are?" I said.

"Than what?" Hewa inquired

"Nothing" I replied "Than we tell those gals, last night we cleanup the room, we believe you're forgot somethings in the boss's room, it was on his bed" I said sarcastically

"Shut up" said Hewa , so we start chuckling

"Maybe tonight we end-up having wet dreams" I said, then we continued laughing, than I sniffed my hands "It's clean now" I said smiling

"Fucking idiot. Why does he keep them under his bed?"

"You never know," said Hewa. "Maybe he wears them during the night."

"We better show them to his son, so he knows what his father is doing here behind his mom," I suggested.

"Don't be stupid," said Hewa. "We're going to lose our jobs; besides, he's still his son."

"But maybe he doesn't know his father's behavior," I said. "You think he does?"

"I don't know; I doubt it," replied Hewa.

"What time is it now?" I asked.

Hewa glanced at his watch. "10:40."

"Do you think he will be back tonight?"

"You never know. It depends."

"When are you going to go to bed?" I asked.

"I'm not sleepy now," said Hewa, "If you are, go to bed."

I got in the bed, and Hewa stood at his place with *The Black Flower* in his hand. Finally, he walked out through the door and sat on the chair in the corridor. He opened the book and started reading first story.

In My Dream

I put my luggage on the floor, started collecting my clothes, then put them back in the luggage quickly. I left the room, stepped out into the living room, and entered the kitchen. I was making sure the gas stove was off. I popped open the head of the gas bottle to be sure. I switched off the refrigerator and opened its door. I took out all the food and put it in a plastic bag. I also dumped all the water containers in the kitchen sink. I scanned the rooms quickly, shut all the doors, and walked around the house, making sure all the windows were closed and everything was in the proper place.

I took my luggage and left the house, shutting the door behind me. A truck stopped in front of the house and waited for me. I threw my luggage in the back of the truck and climbed in; the truck began moving. I looked at my house as I leaned back, and I thought about Hewa—when we'd sat together in the back of the truck every time we went out on duty. I closed my eyes and breathed in the cool air. After a short ride, the truck stopped for fuel from one of the fuel sellers on the sidewalk. The driver asked the boy who was selling the fuel, "Is your fuel clean?"

"Sure it is," the boy said. "I'm not giving bad fuel to my customers."

"Okay, then, put twenty liters in the tank for me," said the driver.

After the driver paid for the fuel, he got back in the car and continued driving, He paid no attention to me. I was still sitting in the back, without changing my position. The truck bumping along on the curvy road made my body move uncontrollably, like a lentil boiling in the pot. Finally, I made some move and changed my position. My lower back hurt from crashing against the hard metal.

We turned away from the road to the narrow alley. I had no idea why the driver came to this alley. As far as I knew there was not a soul I knew from our village living in this alley. Finally, the truck stopped in front of a house. Its door clicked open, even before the driver got out from the truck and knocked on the door. I didn't paid much attention, but then, what I heard shocked me—it was the sound of my sweetheart, Talar. I didn't believe my ears at first, but then there was no doubt that was Talar's voice. I turned my head and saw Talar in a white dress, like a bride would wear. She was carrying a little gift, like a roped candy box, and handed it to the driver. She didn't say anything to me and didn't even look at me—it was as if I didn't exist. Finally, Talar went back to the house without a word and closed the door behind her.

I was looking at her all this time without saying a word. No matter how hard I tried, my lips didn't move--they felt frozen in place. My eyes were fixed on her, but the words wouldn't come out. The truck began to move, and I fixed my eyes on the house, confused. Gradually, the door of the house became smaller and smaller and finally all the house vanished in a white mist, even though it was daytime.

I wanted to find out what was in that box she handed to the driver. I turned my head toward the driver and asked, "What's in that box she handed to you?"

"It's none of your business," he replied,

I was about to punch him in the face, when he hit the brakes as a little boy ran in front of the truck suddenly. My chest was crushed on the truck, and my hand loosened from the metal tool I was holding. I fell back and my head hit the bottom of the truck. Blood gushed from my head, covering the surface of the white truck. My eyes rolled in a very fast speed, like characters in the kids' movies.

When I opened my eyes, I was on the floor, face up. I saw a little spider walking on the ceiling. The light was on, and Brwa was in the room. He opened the refrigerator door, tilted his head when I hit the floor, and shouted, "Lord! Are you okay?" He came forward quickly—and then I found out that I had been dreaming.

Brwa gave me a hand and checked the back of my head. I started scratching my head. A very sharp pain went through my body, and my head felt heavy. Brwa poured some water in a glass and held it out to me.

"Thank you so much," I said after drinking the water.

"You better lie down on the floor. You can move the mattress if you want."

"I had a bad dream," I told him.

"You fell down in your dream?" Brwa inquired.

"Yeah, that's what happened," I replied, grimacing.

"Your dream came true right away," he said, chuckling. "Your going to be fine."

"It was awful!" I scratched my head.

"I had a dream like that once, but luckily, I was asleep on the floor so I didn't get hurt like you did," said Brwa. "I fell off a bicycle in my dream."

"What time is it now?" I asked him.

"About 1:30. How long have you been asleep?"

"It was about 10:30 when I went to bed," I replied. "Where's Hewa?"

"He went home," said Brwa. "Are you dreaming of him?"

"Went home?" I asked worriedly.

"Yeah, they called him. His mom's not feeling well again, so he had to go home."

"So you mean Hewa went to take her to the hospital?" I asked.

"Yeah, probably he took her to emergency," replied Brwa.

"Who drove him home?" I asked.

"No one," he replied. "He rented a taxi."

"That's not good," I said.

I took my rifle and went outside, sitting on the empty chair beside Dyari.

Hewa didn't come back that night. I later learned that he'd taken his mom to the emergency room, and they hospitalized her right away.

I Meet the Girls in the Bus Station

I was standing outside the house before sunrise. I was hungry so I ate some rice and soup. I had a couple cigars in my pocket that I'd bought the previous evening. I lit one of them now and sat on a chair, gazing at the empty alley. Brwa and Dyari had been standing outside, but when I came out, they went back in. It seemed they had a private matter to discuss. So I sat alone on the chair with my rifle on my lap. I rethought the plan I had with Hewa last evening. I glanced at my watch and saw it was 5:15 in the morning. "In couple hours, the sun will rise," I told myself. "I doubt we'll be able to come back this afternoon to see those gals."

Then I realized I should check the room to see if Hewa left the book. I tossed the butt of my cigar under my foot and went back in the house to the guards room. Dyari was sitting alone, and the book *The Black Flower* was in his hand. He was busy with reading.

"Oh, Hewa left the book?" I asked.

"Is that his book?" Dyari inquired.

"Yes, it is."

"Did you want it?" he asked.

"Oh, no, you can read it," I replied.

He put it back on his lap and continued reading.

"Do you think Hewa's mom's condition is a serious one? Did he say anything when he left?" I asked Dyari.

"I don't know for sure," Dyari replied, marking his index finger between the pages. "He just said his mom was in the hospital so he had to go."

"So she was already in the hospital?" I said.

"I guess so," replied Dyari.

"I will call him on my way home to see how his mom doing. We're best friends."

"I see," said Dyari. He stood and handed the book to me. "I hope everything works out for him."

"Why don't you read it?" I asked him.

"No, I didn't mean to read all the stories. I just saw it here"

"You can read it whenever you want," I said, putting the book on the small table in the corner of the room.

As I left the room, Brwa came out from the bathroom, washed his hand, and then laid down on his back and closed his eyes. I grabbed a book and went back to my seat. I'd read a few when I heard the sound of cars stopping in front of the house. The government official was coming back home after two weeks' journey from the border of the country. It was about six-thirty in the morning. Our friends who'd gone with him got out of the cars.

"Good morning, guys," said the government official M to us, and we welcomed him back warmly, even though none of us liked him in our hearts. M went inside with our leader, and after a while, all the guards gathered when the guards leader came out. "He's taking a rest. If anyone asks, let them know he will not be available until late afternoon," our leader informed us.

I went home after sunrise. Because Hewa had left early last night, I had no companion on my way home, so I was alone with the rifle hanging on my shoulder. I walked along the alley and people came out from their homes, heading to work. Students walked to school. I saw groups of high school girls on my way and enjoyed watching them, but I had my mind always on my sweetheart, Talar. All the girls in the world didn't compare to her in my sight. "I'm deeply in love with you, the angel of my life," I whispered to myself like a madman. When I reached the bus stop, I saw a group of girls waiting for bus to arrive. One of them was dressed very sexy, and was calling someone on her cell phone. She was waiting for someone to pick up at the other end, and I couldn't move my eyes away from her as she impatiently clicked a pen in her hand.

"Hi, Mom," she finally said. "Do you know today is Thursday? That's why I'm calling you," she said. Then she spoke in a low tone that I couldn't hear and finally said good-bye. She put the cell phone back in her purse and tilted her head toward her friends. "I let her know," she said. "So, you still keeping that promise?" she asked one of her friends.

"Yeah, I will," her friend replied, "as long as you are by my side.

"I'm sure you going to love it," said the sexy-looking girl.

"Is it close?" asked her friend.

"Yeah, just around the corner, from here" she replied. "Not now, though; later afternoon."

When the bus arrived finally, they hurried on and I followed them. They sat down in two empty seats beside each other, other one sat across on their right side, and I sat right in front of them. I put my rifle between my legs, took out my cell phone, and started going through my incoming and outgoing calls, giving myself the appearance of being busy so they wouldn't realize I was listening to their conversation. I had a gut feeling that they might be those girls who went to the boss's house,

"It's like you're reborn," said the sexy girl to her friend.

"Don't talk about; we're on the bus," said her friend, and she was chuckling.

"When you try it once, you want to talk about it everywhere," she went on.

"You better end it now," her friend demanded.

"There are not many people on the bus," she said, but her friend didn't reply.

They were quit for a while, then the sexy gril tell her friend "I believe he's working for M" now they're talking about me, but since I'm not sure and they're sat behind me I pretending that I don't know who they talk about it, but her friend reply was "Sh..sh..sh" then sexy one said "I have something I will show you later."

"What is it?" her friend asked, but she didn't reply. "Why you don't you show me now?"

"As I said, later," she assured her "You will need to use it this afternoon".

The bus stopped at all the stations and picked up more passengers on the way. The girls started talking about school, and they got off at the next stop, but I decided not to follow them. Instead, it came to my mind to change my seat to the seats where they had been sitting. When I sat down on the sexy girl's seat, I looked at my rifle to make sure its belt wasn't tucked on anything, and when I moved my feet, I felt something under my left foot. I reached out for it. It was a little square bag, face down and unopened. I pick it up and felt it; no doubt it was a condom. I put it in my pocket. No one noticed, of course. Then I remember M's bedroom.

When the bus reached the final destination, I got off and decided to call Hewa, to see how his mom was doing. He sounded sleepy when he answered. "I'm sorry to bother you," I said. "I just want to know your mom's condition."

"Thank you so much. God rewards you," Hewa replied. "I haven't slept yet. The doctor said she should be under treatment until she recovers."

"I'm sorry to hear that," I said. "If you need anything, don't hesitate to contact me."

"I appreciate your concern," said Hewa.

"By the way," I said, "if she needs blood, my blood type is A+. I can give it in case of emergency; just let you know."

"The doctor hasn't mentioned anything like that. Hopefully, she'll get better soon. Please pray for her."

"Sure, I will. I hope she recovers soon. Have they said what's wrong with her?" I asked.

"They don't know yet," Hewa explained. "They gave her a blood test and said that her blood pressure is little low, but they didn't give any further explanation."

"We all pray for her," I said.

"Thank you," Hewa replied.

"Do you think you will make it for the plan we had?" I asked.

"You know my situation, but I'll try my best."

"I understand. I don't mean to bother you," I said. "I will come to the hospital later this afternoon. We can see what's best. If not today, we will do it next Thursday. We have all the time in world. Hopefully your mom will recover, with the help of God."

"Hopefully, she will," said Hewa.

I Meet Hewa in the Hospital

The howling, sharp sound of the cart driver in the alley—selling tomatoes, cucumbers, eggplants, zucchini, fresh onions, celery, leeks—close to my house woke me up. That was followed by the screaming of a bunch of kids, playing and shouting close by. When I glanced at my watch, it was only twelve-thirty.

"I'm not working today," I said to myself, "but I have to visit Hewa at the hospital. I can sleep early tonight." Since I started living on my own, I developed the habit of talking to myself around the house,

I got out of bed, went to the bathroom, and washed my face. After that, I got some cheese and a bowl of sour cream from the refrigerator. Then I put the kettle on for tea and grabbed my cell phone to check my incoming calls. There was a call from Hewa, so I dialed his number. It rang several times and then a woman answered.

"Can I speak with Hewa?" I said.

"Hewa went out, brother, but he will be back shortly," replied the woman.

"May I ask to whom am I speaking?" I inquired.

"I stayed with his mom last night," she replied without introducing herself.

"I'm Rebeen, his friend," I said. "Can you please let him know I called when he comes back?"

"Rebeen?" she inquired.

"Yes, Rebeen."

"Sure, I will," she said.

"So how's his mom's condition?" I asked.

"She's better now. Thank you for asking."

"I pray for her." I said, before saying good-bye.

The water was at a full boil by then, and I added some tea bags for ten minutes. When it was ready, I put a couple spoons of sugar in my glass and poured in some tea. I took out the bread, cut a slice of it, dipped in the cream, and put it in my mouth. I poured another tea as soon as I finished the first one, then slurped it down. After I finished my breakfast, I washed the tea glass and sour cream cup.

I went to change my clothes and comb my hair and then went outside. It was a nice day—the sky was clear and it wasn't too hot. A cool breeze was blowing. When I reached the bus station, I changed my mind and decided to walk to the hospital. I walked along the sidewalk, past the plaza close to my house—most of them have little grocery shops or snack shops. There also was one mechanic and an auto shop among them, with a blacksmith shop and a barber shop down the street. Since I'd lived in the area for almost ten years, I used to shop around often. I bought my breads every other day in the bakery shop. I always went to that barber shop when I wanted a haircut, and I bought groceries from those shops. Even my mom, before she decided to go back to the village, also shopped at this plaza., When I was a child, I spent my daily money my mom gave me at those snack shops, buying my favorite candy.

Half an hour later, I arrived at the hospital. I decided to call Hewa on his cell phone to see if he was still there, and then I bought a box of candy from one a souvenir seller in front of the hospital for his mom.

Hewa answered his phone on the first ring.

"Hi, I called you a while ago," I said.

"Yeah, I know; my aunt told me she talked to you," he replied,

"So which room is your mom in?" I asked. "I'm at the main gate right now."

"Stay there," Hewa said, "I'll come down and get you in a minute." Shortly, he arrived and let the gatekeeper know that I was his friend, and he kindly let me in. Hewa took me to his mom's room on the third floor. She was lying on her bed, and a woman was sitting by her side on the chair.

Should be her sister, I guessed, because Hewa had referred to her as his aunt. She was feeding Hewa's mom.

"How are you, Mom?" I said.

"Welcome, my son," she replied.

"I pray God gives you a cure soon," I said. "I'm really sorry for what I heard."

"God save you from all kind of harm with my Hewa and folks' children," she praised me. Hewa left the room then, and I followed him after excusing myself. We sat down beside each other. His mother had lost a lot of weight, and her color was pale, but I didn't mention that to Hewa.

"What's the doctor said?" I asked him.

"They don't know yet," Hewa commented. "She's to stay here for treatment, until we see her condition improving."

"May Lord give her mercy, and she gets back on her feet," I said. We were quiet for a while, and then I said, "Seems like you're not going to make it to work today."

"I'm afraid not," he replied. "My aunt's here. My brother and my sisters are all coming later."

"But that's not what I meant," I said. "I meant our plan to visit."

"Oh, right. I already forgot about it."

"You forgot already?" I asked.

"If you hate anyone, just wish to see them in the situation I'm in," said Hewa.

"Yeah, I know. It's hard. I don't blame you," I said in a melancholy voice. "I'm sorry; we can cancel it if you like. The book you brought in is already there, though. I put it in a drawer."

"Oh, good," he said. "I'll try to make an excuse, and we will go shortly."

"As you wish," I said. "If you think you can't, just forget it; we can go next week."

"No, that's okay," Hewa assured me.

"I also have a something else to tell you," I said. " You're not going to believe it."

"What is it?"

"It's also about them. I believe I saw them this morning in the bus station."

"You saw whom?"

"Those gals!" I explained.

"How? They were at the bus station?" Hewa asked eagerly.

"Yes, they were there when I came back home."

"How are you so sure they were those gals?" Hewa inquired.

"I listened to their conversation, and based on that, they are going to visit the boss today, after school."

"What did they say?"

I repeated the conversation I'd heard to Hewa and told him that when the girls got off the bus, I changed my seat and found something where they'd been sitting. I took it out the condom I found in the bus from my pocket and held it out to Hewa.

"Man, it's a condom." said Hewa . " Where did you get that"

"I found it in the bus, under their seat when they leave" I explained

"How did you now they were the boss's girls?" Hewa inquired

"Base on what they talk about, she told her friend when she ask if the place close, she said just around the corner from here, and said not now later afternoon, also she said I believe he's working for M, I was the only one work for M who's in that bus"

"Now everything clear who they are?" said Hewa.

"That's why I'm sure," I said. "So what are you going to do now?"

"I will come; there's no doubt," said Hewa.

"Well, it's almost two o'clock," I told him. "We better hurry up."

"Just give me a minute" he said.

He walked back to the room to let his aunt know he was going somewhere with me. Then we both left the hospital and walked on toward the street. He was singing some songs, quietly.

"You think it's better go by bus or rent a taxi?" I asked.

"Either way is fine with me," Hewa said.

We stopped on the edge of the sidewalk and a taxi appear shortly. I held my hand up for it to stop. We jumped in and let the driver know where to go. We didn't say much to each other while we were in the taxi. Fifteen minutes later, we reached the area. We let the driver know we wanted to get off before he entered the alley. I paid the driver, and we walked toward the house. Three of the guards—Dyari, Aras, and Awat—were seated outside under the shade of the berry tree. Its branches came out over the wall.

Dyari was seated on the cement bench by the fence wall of the house. They looked at us suspiciously—they knew we had the day off. When we got closer, Awat asked, "What are you guys doing here?"

"Hewa left a book here last night," I responded. "We just came to get it."

"Yeah, that's why I came back," Hewa agreed. "I borrowed it from a friend, and he wants it back."

"Well, something happened to his book," said Awat. "When we're ate our lunch, Aras was leafing through its pages, and he spilled a bowl of soup on the book. We tried our best to clean it, but it's still wet."

"You're kidding me!" Hewa said.

"I'm not kidding. Go and see for yourself. It's on the table," Awat assured him. Hewa walked inside, but they called him back.

"Hey, hold on, we're kidding," Awat said.

Hewa stopped short. "Well, I'm still going to get it."

"No, come back," said Aras in a low tone.

"Why ?" Hewa asked.

They smiled and signaled him by hand to come back. "He has a guest inside; that's why we're out here," Aras explained.

"What kind of guest ?" Hewa wanted to know.

Aras moved his left hand while holding his rifle with his right, the way a man moves his hand when masturbating. "You get it?"

"You're not serious? Are you?" asked Hewa, surprised.

"You can wait if you wish, until they come out," said Awat.

I tilted my head toward Awat. "When did they arrive?"

"Over an hour, I guess," Awat replied.

"So that's what happens every Thursday?" I asked them.

"Kind of," said Dyari.

"What a life were stuck with," I said. "So how long we should remain withis job?"

"What did you mean?" Hewa inquired.

"Don't you guys ever think about, if one day M get catch he will be punish, we are also guilty, because we are guarding his ass."

"It's his house and besides, we're not involved or responsible for what's going on in there while the owner is at home," said Dyari.

"What if their families found out and followed them here?" I asked. "We're not here to guard his ass? We're in charge of all the opposition this house faces, so that means it might even cost us our lives someday. I'm serious, guys; it's a dangerous zone."

"What did you say? You're a kid. You don't understand the world yet, When are you going to grow up?" Aras inquired.

"You think nothing's going to happen if he continues that way?" I inquired.

"No, because if the girls came from respectable families, they wouldn't end up in here every week. It's their bodies; they can do anything with it. It's their choice so who cares?" said Aras.

I shrugged "I'm still concerned for us."

"You can't stop anyone from what they desire to do; that's about it," said Awat.

The living room door clicked open from inside. Two girls appeared in school uniforms. "Here they are," said Aras as they came down the steps of the little front deck of the house. After they walked through the passageway, they came into view in front of us. They paid no attention to us as they passed by "How's your examination Zeno?" asked other gril to the sexy-looking gril, "Fine" she replied. They bent their heads down, I could not see any change on the face of the sexy one—who turned-out to be Zeno. She was the one I saw on the bus—but her friend looked bewildered. None of us said a thing; we just looked at them from behind. When they reached the corner of the alley, before they're disappeared from sight, the sexy one known as Zeno tilted her head and looked at us with a smile.

Hewa went to grab his book in the guards room, and when he came out, we left the house. We went to the bus station, returned to the city center, and wandered around until late evening. Then we walked home.

When I awoke on Friday morning around 9:30, I was still feeling tired from the previous day—I hadn't done so much walking in the last four months or so. I made breakfast, cleaned the kitchen after I ate, and then took a quick shower.

I'd arranged with Hewa to meet him around noon at his house, and we went to the market again and stayed at the teahouse for a hour. After that we went to the mosque and attended Friday prayer. The Imam finished Friday speech around two-thirty in the afternoon, and we talked about different things on the way home.

Hewa seemed so upset about the future of our generation and thinking that day after day, people are going astray. "I don't think the future bring any success to our nation, as we hoped for. If prostitution occupies the heads of teenagers, distraction will spread in the city faster than anybody can imagine."

I nodded in agreement, even though I think that in previous years, when we were kids, people were much more aware of the dangers of prostitutions. Nowadays, it's the government seeding this plant, like our boss M, for example. That's worse than outside enemies, in my opinion.

The Beggar Knocks on My Door

I called Hewa the next morning as soon as I woke up. "Today we head back to work again, like good pimps, I guess," I said.

"Indeed, we are, even though it's not our choice. But guarding M for whatever reason is accountable in the public eye," said Hewa.

"Did you dream about the girls?" I inquired.

"Nah, I'm just joking," responded Hewa.

"I'm afraid that one day after he get bored with those whores, he might come and ask us to find him some. What do you think?"

"I think so," said Hewa. "You know, when you get hard, you will do anything to calm it down."

"You just woke up; are you hard in the bed?" I ask amiably.

"Tell you the truth, yes, I am, but when I got your call, it turned me off."

"I'm called you when you were about to cum?" I asked,

"No, my dream wasn't like that," Hewa explained.

"What it was like?"

"Just normal. We were there and they came to the house, like yesterday, and went to his room, and they don't pay any attention to us at all."

"Didn't you have a wet dream?" I asked him.

"No, I didn't" Hewa said frankly.

"Oh, I almost forgot it," I said. "How's your mom's condition now?"

"She's about same; thank you for asking," said Hewa.

"Okay, see you later. I think I might come little bit earlier than usual," I said. "I want to see a friend of mine in the market around two o'clock. He's selling miscellanies on the cart close to the city center."

"He's a carter, you mean?" asked Hewa.

"Yes, he is," I replied,

After I hung up, I thought about Talar. I really wanted to see her. I hadn't talked to her for almost over a week, and I didn't know how to get in touch with her except on her way to school. I start wandering around the house, pacing in the rooms. *She has my number, but probably she hasn't had a chance to contact me*, I thought. I collected my laundry and took it to the bathroom. I found detergent under the kitchen sink, but the power was off. Nowadays during daytime in our city, most areas have this problem; it's became a daily routine. I opened the bathroom door and put my clothes in the little plastic basin to wash them. Then I remembered I had no warm water available. I used it all up on my shower earlier. I left the laundry in the bathroom—I should've washed it earlier. I came outside and found an empty oil container in the passageway at the corner of the house. I filled the container half full of water, and used a little stove to boil the water. Then I returned to the living room to read the book I borrowed from Hewa the other day. I read the first of the six short stories and then went to check on the water—it had warmed up, so I took the hot water to the bathroom and poured some in the basin, then applied some detergent to the water. Piece by piece, I washed my clothes, finishing with my underwear and socks. When I finished collecting them in the plastic bucket and squeezing every piece, I hung them over the wire clothesline to get dry under the sun's heat.

By this time I was hungry—I hadn't had much at breakfast—so I cooked some rice and soup the way I remembered my mom would cook it. I washed my dishes after I finished my lunch, and put what remained in lunch containers for work.

Life seems easy sometimes when you're alone. You are your own boss, but I still dreamed of the day that Talar would cook for me. I thought of her wherever I went, On the other hand, when I thought of those girls and their way of life, a fear occupied me all over. Sometime I even thought that Talar might change her mind and find someone else. "You better think positive," I told myself. My voice echoed in the empty house. I wandered around—when there's no electric power, there's no TV to watch, no music to play. *I better read another story*, I thought.

The weather was chilly so I had the stove on, and I managed my life on my own. *I can take care of a family*, I thought, but of course my mom didn't think I could. She thought I hadn't grown up yet. "Life is challenging; you have to always fight it," I said. I opened the book to the page where I'd stopped reading and began a second story. I'd finished first page when someone knocked on the door. With the book in my hand, I went to the door and saw a very old man in shabby clothes. His voice came out like someone on his death bed. He asked for help; he was a beggar. I felt terrible when I saw him in this condition, and it made me feel so grateful for what I have in my position. I put my hand in my pocket to take out some cash, and the old man start praying for me right away. He began to leave, but I asked, "Are you feel hungry?" He said nothing, but he froze in his place. "Come on in. I have lunch ready," I said.

He stepped in and followed me into the kitchen without a word. I left the outside door open—the alley was quiet; only few passersby from here and there.

"Sit down, please," I said kindly.

He sat on the bunk foam mattress, and I opened the refrigerator door to take out the rice and soup and reheated some on the gas stove. "How old are you, sir?" I asked him.

"Seventy-six," he replied.

"Do you have any family?"

"I have a daughter."

"What about a wife?" I inquired.

"She is dead."

"I am sorry," I said. "How did she die?"

"She died by the bombing plane in the time of war," he reported.

"When was that?" I asked.

"In 1988, during the war," he replied.

"I am sorry," I said glumly.

"Yeah, everybody says that," he said.

I watched him with a faint smile on my lips. I put the food on the tray and presented it to him. He started eating, and I filled a glass of water and handed it to him. He drank it all in one gulp, then gave me back the glass. I poured him another, and he drank that one in the same way. "Alhamdu lilah," he said. "All praise be to the Lord."

I felt happy for him when I saw that he was pleased. "So, what's your daughter doing now, or where is she?" I asked him.

"She's married and lives with her husband," he replied.

"Do they live here?" I asked.

"No, they don't."

"Do you have any place to stay at night?"

"I sleep on the street most times," the old man informed me.

"Does she know your situation?" I inquired.

"Yeah, she knows," he said frankly.

"Why doesn't she help you, then? What kind of daughter is she?" I was really pissed off when I heard that. *Maybe other people don't think like I do*, I thought.

"She's not living in this country," he informed me.

"Where does she live?"

"She went to Iran ten years ago."

"Does she come back to visit you?"

"Never," he said. "She might think I'm long dead."

"What about rest of your family?" I asked. "Do you have any other children?"

"My two sons and other daughter died along with my wife," he said finally.

"At the plane bombing?"

"My daughter and a son, yes," he said. "But my other son was missing. I didn't even recover his body."

"How did he get lost? Or how did you know he's dead and not living somewhere else, like your daughter?"

"He was lost on his way to Europe," he explained. "Bad friends betrayed him to go there; he didn't listen to me. I told him I would find him a wife, but he wouldn't change his mind." He wiped his mouth and dried his tearing eyes. "I had a house, I sold it for him and gave him all the money to get there." I folded my hands on my chest, waiting for him to go on. "I didn't want to break his heart. One day he took the money and left with his friends. That was a last time I saw him. After few months, they said he had been shot by the Turkish army. Only some of the bodies were returned to their families, but my son wasn't among them. I knew he died, but I didn't hold a funeral for him. I have no money left. I couldn't afford it, but I didn't get his body."

"Don't you have any relatives? A brother or sister?"

"Relatives ... brother, sister?" he repeated, shaking his head.

I didn't ask any more questions. I knew that he was deeply wounded—I could see it in his face. I thought about all the money that my boss, M, had, his family and children, but that didn't satisfy him. He looked for whores to sleep with and was after girls the same age as his daughter. I came to the conclusion that the leaders of our country want to betray the new generation, and truth be told, they would like for this nation to become a nation without any rules or conduct. They want to built the paradise for themselves to satisfy their wild desires and leave the rest of the nation in their problems.

The old man finished eating and thanked me a thousand times. I told him not to thank me but to thank and praise the Lord Almighty. He left to go back to his life—the life no one desire to have and I prayed that the Lord would give him a better life.

"I'm so grateful, Lord, for what you gave me—for my life, the wealth I have, and for making me believe in you, and for the respect and honor of my family in the people's eyes."

I start cleaning the kitchen and washing the dishes. By the time I finished I had ninety minutes left before I had to go to work. "Tomorrow we are supposed to get our monthly paycheck," I remembered. I closed all the doors, took my lunchbox, and with *Black Flower* in hand, I left the house.

A Letter from My Mother

I knocked on the door of Hewa's house, and waited for him to come out, Hewa complained that I was early but I reminded him that I wanted to see the carter at the market.

"But you're not going to spend a lot time with him, are you?"

"Of course not. A friend of mine just came back from the village, and he has a letter for me from my mom," I explained. "He couldn't stay long enough to see me, but he gave me the name of this carter and said he'd leave the letter with him. Most of the time he's on the street somewhere in the city center, so now I want to see what was going on, what message my mom has for me."

"I didn't know your mom was educated?" said Hewa, surprised.

"She's not; she's illiterate."

"So, you mean your stepfather wrote the letter?" Hewa asked me.

"Yes, he did."

"Do you call him mom, too?" Hewa teased.

"You're making fun of everything; you are a jerk."

"Then we will go, I'll follow until you get there; after that, you follow me." Hewa kept joking.

"Yeah, right," I said hurriedly. "Let's go."

"Of course," said Hewa, "Your mom handed you to me, so I have to make sure of your safety, until I return you to her the way she sent you to the city."

"Why? Do you think I'm a little kid or what?"

"Not only that, but also I want you to have a good appetite and gain some weight," he added.

"Do you think I'm a sheep, cow, or some kind of cattle to put on more weight?" I said jokingly.

He burst out in a big laugh but then we remained silent for a while. Finally, Hewa said, "Why didn't this guy just leave the letter with your neighbor?"

"Good question," I said. "I can't tell you; maybe he didn't want to give the letter to someone he doesn't know."

By the time we reached the market border, a lot of carters were wandering along the street.

"Where are you supposed to find him?" Hewa asked.

"Somewhere around here, where all carts are gathered," I said. "Sometimes he's roaming around."

"So you're not quite sure where he is?" asked Hewa.

"No, but I can spot him," I said. "He always wears a hat like those a shepherd wears. Most of the time he rolls his sleeves to his elbows."

"Oh, I see, he's like a cowboy, then," said Hewa.

"You can say that."

"But he's not a cowboy; he's a cart-boy," said Hewa, mockingly.

"Yeah, that's right, and I will tell him when we meet him."

"Go ahead; I'll tell him to his face," Hewa replied, seeming like he didn't care at all.

After some searching, we were not able to find him. I almost gave hope.

"You said he roams around the streets," Hewa reminded me.

"Yeah, he does."

"So you think you'll find him on this busy market, just by chance?" Hewa asked gloomily.

"Yes, why not?"

"You are losing your mind if you think you'll find him here," said Hewa. "And we don't have much time left. We're going to be late."

Suddenly, he came into view from nowhere. I walked toward him, waving my hand across the street. His cart was parked on our side, but he seemed to coming back from somewhere else.

"I had the letter for you this morning. I thought you would show up in the morning!" he shouted to me as he crossed the street.

"How are you, Kak Wali?" I said as we shook hands. He also shook hands with Hewa. "He's Kak Hewa," I introduced him. They greeted each other, and then Kak Wali put his hand in his pants pocket and took out a letter. "Here's your letter," he said, handing it to me.

"Thanks a lot," I said.

"Any time," Kak Wali responded kindly.

"Well, I'm almost late for work. I have to go. I will read it and see what they want."

"You're going to work, you said?" asked Kak Wali. "What do you do?"

"I am a guard," I informed him.

"You are a guard?" Kak Wali seemed interested to hear me say that.

"Yes, I am," I assured him. "Don't you see my rifle?"

"Sure, my eyes still can see. I'm not that old to have lost my sight."

"I am glad to hear that," I said.

"I just wondered what you did when I saw your rifle," Kak Wali went on. "Where are you a guard? What company or administration?"

"Not a company or administration," I said. "A government official's house."

"Who's that government official?" Kak Wali inquired.

When I said M's name, he shook his head and gave me a smiling look without saying anything.

"Why do you look at me like that? Is that anything wrong?" I inquired.

"I've heard the folks talk about him, how he behaves," said Kak Wali.

"What do you mean by that?"

"They say he doesn't spend a night without a woman."

"Yeah, that's what I heard, too, but that's not my problem," I explained. "Besides, whoever has power and position like him does the same. Anyone who is not like him, I believe, just doesn't know how to do it."

"True enough. You better go so you're not late, and make sure to send your mom whatever she asked for in the letter."

"Okay, good-bye for now, and thanks for the letter."

"How does he know about our boss's behavior?" Hewa asked me after we left.

"I'm as surprised as you are that he knows about the boss," I said honestly. "I believe folks see us as pimps because they see better than what we see."

"I think we better start looking for other jobs somewhere else," Hewa suggested.

"That's what I said the other day, but here we are, heading back to that whorehouse." I shrugged when Hewa didn't respond. "What about Thursday? We can look for other jobs on Thursday if we really want to."

"Oh, really? So from now on, you're not going to see your sweetheart on Thursday so we can look for other jobs?" Hewa asked.

"Well, I don't know. Let's if he's been there today or not," I said.

"There's a bus—hold your hand out for it."

The Problem of My Friend with His Father

Sitting on the bus without saying a word, we both gazed out the window in the same direction. Along the road, people walked past shops, and here and there were the cart drivers, loaded with goods. Most of the shops were open now, except for newly built shops still available for rent.

I checked my pocket for my ID card with my guard badge; then I shoved it back into my pocket. Then I checked my breast pocket where I had a folded paper. It had an address written on it but no name. I hadn't noticed it until that moment—the other day one of my friends gave it to me and told me to visit him when I got a chance.

Maybe he is still waiting for me to show up on his door, I thought. That was a four months ago. I'd left that shirt on the hanger in my closet when we went to the village last summer. Maybe he wondered where I've been all this time. I thought to call him but didn't have his number.

"What's that?" Hewa asked when he saw the paper in my hand.

"It's the address of a friend I had in elementary school," I told Hewa "I saw him about four months ago, and he gave me his address, but then I moved to the village and forgot about it."

"Do I know him?" Hewa inquired.

"I'm afraid you don't," I replied. "He's a nice guy, though, just like yourself, but he also has some family problems. He told me about it when we met that day."

"What kind of problems?" Hewa inquired.

"The guy has a bad relationship with his father," I said. "Not that his father is a bad guy, but he told me they haven't gotten along with each other since he was a little boy. Whenever he played soccer with his friends when he was a kid, his mother told his father about it when he got home from work in the evening, and then his father would beat him for it. But my friend never gave up soccer." The bus make a stop and most of the passengers got off. We changed our spots for better seats. "Now he's playing for a soccer team, but his father doesn't pay him any attention. Also, my friend is in love with a girl, and they've been together for almost two years now. He wants to get married, but his father won't help him at all. He said that his father told him that he would never ask anyone to hand his daughter to my friend in marriage, not unless he gave up his 'stupid game.' I told him to agree with his father until he got the girl, and then later he could go back to his game."

Hewa nodded as he checked his watch. We got off at the bus station and walked toward the house.

"My friend agreed with my suggestion," I went on. "He was asked me to go with him and talk to his father about it—that's why he gave me his address back then, but I just remembered now, when I checked my pocket on the bus."

"Maybe he's still waiting for you," said Hewa. "This world of ours is full of weird situations."

"Maybe he's still trying with his father. I don't even have his phone number or any way to contact him."

"What is his name?" Hewa inquired.

"His name is Dana," I replied.

"Why don't you just visit him sometime? See how he's doing," Hewa suggested.

"Yeah, that's what I think too."

We were almost to the house when we saw a few kids playing on the other end of the alley. They were shouting at each other, and from one of the houses, a beautiful girl poked her head out from the door, checking both sides of the alley. We gazed at her for few seconds, and then she went back into the house, slamming the door.

The Day the Boss Got the Phone Call

That evening, after we reached the boss's house, the sky was cloudy and it looked like it would rain later on, but none of us had an umbrella. When we went to the shop a few blocks away at our break time, the drops of rain tapping over us soaked our clothes. We walked faster than usual to get the house, and in the alley, we saw M in his car. He seemed to be going out somewhere. M was seated in front, by the driver, with two guards in the backseat, The two guards waved their hands at us, and we waved back. The boss was looking at us as he talked on the phone, but he didn't make any signal to us. The expression on his face looked as if he was in a deep depression.

"Maybe something urgent happened, related to war on the country or something," I said. M was one of the skilled commanders of war. I was right—something urgent had occurred, but we didn't know what it was.

"Maybe his son got in some sort of trouble," Hewa said.

Since we didn't hear anything in the news about a big opposition facing the country, I agreed with Hewa.

When we entered the house, the guards leader Awat was talking to the other guards. They were standing in the corridor and talking about the situation that had recently happened. We still had no clue what was going on, but soon after, Awat announced that he was going to go, and he advised us to follow Shorrsh. He decided we should obey him and told him to discuss the matter with us before he made any decisions. Then he left the house, saying, "Call me if you get new information!"

We gathered around Shorrsh and asked, "What are we supposed to do? What is going on?"

Shorrsh hesitated for a while. "What should I do now?" Shorrsh said worriedly. He turned to face Brwa, but Brwa didn't say anything. All the guards sank into silence, so we did too. We didn't hear anything except of the sound of rain. Shorrsh headed back to the living room, and we followed him without a word. "Don't leave this door for now," Shorrsh ordered. "If they come for him now and attack, they will kill all of us. What does he care if we die for his mistake?" Shorrsh announced bitterly.

"I'm not putting my life in danger for something disgraceful," said Aras ."He's the one who put our lives at risk, and he ran."

I checked my rifle to make sure I had it fully loaded with bullets; Hewa did the same.

"He went to fix the mess, not run," said Shorrsh.

"Did he give them back their virginity?" Sardar asked sarcastically.

"We may get some results before dark," Shorrsh announced. "Besides, we better stay here tonight—none of us leave."

"What's the difference? Nothing changes what was happened," Dyari said, and we understood then that his net got caught.

"It makes a difference," I said. "At least we're all going to see if he's punished."

"Why should we get punished for his mistake?" Hewa ask worriedly.

"I'm afraid we'll also end up in court," said Shorrsh frankly.

"For what reason? Why would we pay the price of his mistake? None of us slept with them. I don't even know their names," said Hewa.

"I'm just joking," said Shorrsh. "Besides, I'm not saying he's innocent, but trust me: most of the government officials do much worse than he did, but they are lucky. They haven't been caught like him. We all know that if government cared, no one could open a whorehouse in the city."

"That's true enough," said Aras.

"But why do we get punished? We didn't find them or bring them for him," Hewa kept asking.

"You don't get it: I said *if* he ends up in court. Do you understand now?" Shorrsh asked.

"I see," said Hewa.

"But the question is, how did they find out about him today?" I inquired.

"Don't ask me; he didn't tell us anything, and that is not important now. He was so confused that he put his clothes on in the blink of an eye. He got ready and took his relative driver with him—what was his name?" Shorrsh asked.

"Renas," replied Aras.

"Yeah, him, and he took poor Hawzen with Rebaz also," said Shorrsh. "Anyway Rebaz a guard just like us, but Hawzen know how to cook for him, besides we don't know how he found out."

"Maybe one of them got pregnant," said Aras. "He was fucking them like a donkey."

"We don't know anything yet," Shorrsh warned. "We shouldn't make any statement or start rumors based on false information."

The government official M went to see his best friend, right after he got the call from someone who was in a higher position—sometimes they shared women on different occasions—to help him find some salvation for what happened to him. M didn't tell any of the guards except the leader, whom he trusted, but all the guards knew right away when he got the phone call, judging by the words M spat out angrily.

Shorrsh began tell us what had happened before we came. He said that when M was on the phone, he heard M insist that he hadn't "forced them" and that they "came voluntarily." He insisted to the person on the phone that the girls all asked when they could come back, and M finished by saying, "I swear on my honor."

I was about to burst out in a big laugh when I learned he'd said that. M listened to the person on the phone and from time to time said things like, "I understand" and "I have nothing to fear." Shorrsh said that M kept insisting that he didn't force anyone to do anything she didn't want to do. "They're young, I know, but they chose to be here," he'd said. Finally, it came out that the principal of the high school had called the police. M's response to that was to say, "Why didn't that bitch call me first?"

I was again about to burst into a big laugh. I almost had to leave the room. Shorrsh finished his story by telling us that M listened to the other person on the line for five minutes on the phone, and M was all ears for that time. Then he agreed to "come down and discuss things," but when M got in the car, he started making phones calls—Shorrsh thought it was probably other friends in the government, That was when Hewa and I arrived a while ago.

The Day a Girl Became Unconscious

That day at noon when the bell rang at school, all the students collected their books in the classroom, copybooks along with their pencils and their book bags, and the teachers all left classes to go the school office. The school principal, St. Rwpak, was in office. Most of the students remained in the hallway, though some were out in the schoolyard. Some went to the cafeteria, and some of them stayed in their classes and talked with their schoolmates about the upcoming examinations or their scores. Breaks usually took about ten minutes, and they had four different classes each day, with three short breaks between them. The only day off they had was Friday, like every other government office. Also, almost every high school had two shifts—one that started in the morning around seven o'clock, and the next one that started at noon to five o'clock. Students took their last break around 11:10 for ten minutes.

Zeno and her friends—the two girls she took with her to the government official M's in pervious months—walked in the hallway on their break. They looked around to hunt for some girls she had in her mind for a while.

"She is like a pistachio," Zeno said to Deren and Shler, tilting her head to one girl standing by the wall. "But I'm not sure if she'd listen to me."

"Why is he asking you for new girls?" Shler inquired,

"M always asks for more," Zeno replied. "He wants to make a group of us his own."

"He has a big one, and it works good," Deren said.

"Yeah, I bet you missed it," Zeno said. "Once a week, that's all we have."

They went to the cafeteria, and each bought a sandwich and a drink. They ate quickly, before their break was over, and by the time they finished, they had only two minutes left to get back to class.

"We're almost late!" Shler announced.

"That doesn't matter," said Zeno. "What's important is that we're not late in getting to his school classes."

"I'm afraid I'll get pregnant," said Deren.

"Don't you take the birth control pills M gave to us?" Zeno asked worriedly.

"I do, but I'm still worried," Deren explained. "I afraid it might not work."

"Yes, it works, if you use it like we told you," Zeno assured her. "Do you have your period regularly?"

"Yes, I do, but I don't know—I'm just scared," said Deren.

"Me, too, sometimes," said Shler.

"Awaz said don't worry; it's never going to happen. I'll take care of that," Zeno informed them.

"It feels so nice when he's inside me," said Deren.

"You mean when you're under him," said Zeno.

"We're almost late; hurry up!" Shler warned them. They walked out of the cafeteria and went back to class.

"What class do we have? I forget," Zeno said.

"We have English class," they replied.

"I can't think of anything else when they said today is Thursday," Zeno explained.

"So you didn't understand those classes we had today?" Deren inquired.

"No, I didn't," Zeno said. "I always think about his hard penis, when he shoves inside me. It make me wee-wee when I think about it."

"Seems like the teacher is not in class yet," Shler said when she saw the other girls walking in and out of class, carelessly.

"So we can go home early today," said Deren.

"No, we don't go home. I should take both of you to his house," Zeno said.

"I can't come this week. I'm feeling sick today," Shler informed Zeno.

"Me, too. I have my period," Deren said.

"He called Awaz yesterday and told her that I should take one of you to him if I don't get a new girl," Zeno explained.

"Why doesn't Awaz herself go, then?" Shler inquired.

"She was there Monday," Zeno informed them.

"She can go back today, too, couldn't she?" Shler asked.

"No, Awaz doesn't like to be seen too much by the folks," Zeno said. "Besides, she's going late at night most of the time and spends the night there."

"Did you ever spend a night there with him?" Deren inquired.

"Only once," Zeno replied. "The week M took my virginity."

"So you shared together with your mom?" they inquired.

"No, separate," Zeno explained. "First, he called me, and after a couple hours, he let me go and called her in until the morning."

"You stayed in his house?" they asked.

"Yes, but I just slept after that," Zeno replied.

"What about your mom?" Deren inquired,

"She slept with him in his room," said Zeno.

"So he didn't do it with you after that?" Shler asked.

"Yeah, we did it in the morning before we went home," said Zeno.

"When did you go home that morning?" Shler asked.

"Around ten o'clock," Zeno replied.

"He did it in front of your mom?" Shler kept asking.

"Yeah, of course she was in the room," Zeno said frankly.

"Your mom watched you?" they asked.

"Of course," Zeno said.

"With a condom?" Deren inquired.

"No, not a condom," Zeno said.

"So he cum inside you?" they asked.

"No, he took it out," Zeno informed them. "But one day, he did it with me in the back. I had a lot pain when he was inside me. I forgot my underwear that day," Zeno explained.

"Really?" they inquired. "When did that happen?"

"It was last month," Zeno replied. "Yeah, it was nice after all. That was my first experience in the back."

"Let's talk about something else," Shler said.

"Talk about asking some girl," Zeno suggested.

"We're not going to ask anyone. You go ahead," said Shler.

"I will," Zeno said with certainty. "Until now, I asked anyone to M's house you're included; they're all eager to come with me. Who don't like to have some fun?"

"Maybe she's not. How are you so sure?" Zeno's friends inquired.

"I bet she will, espcially someone like M, he's rich and famous" Zeno said proudly. "Who doesn't like it? Everyone does. You did, when I asked."

"So who do you have in mind?" they asked.

"I'll pick one later, before we go home," Zeno replied.

Other students were talking in groups, and they were whispering all this time. Suddenly, a teacher came to the class and called all the students to go to the other class for geography, because the English teacher called in sick. Finally, all the students went to the other class and also had history and math later that day. They joined with other classes as well, but before math class started, they took their last break. Then Zeno got a chance to talk to the girl she had in mind to invite to government official M's house.

While the girl was studying with three of her friends, Zeno walked up and said, "Hi, what are you guys doing?"

"We're studying math. We have a examination tomorrow morning," they explained.

"Oh, yeah," Zeno said.

A few times before, Zeno talked about sex with her friends, but she never mentioned what she was up to. Up to that point, Zeno never said anything about what was in her mind, but her friends thought she was kind of a lusty girl. When Zeno told them in recent months how she satisfied herself in the bath with vegetables or other objects, she also mentioned that she sent dirty text messages on her cell phone to some boys she met on her way to school.

"May I ask you a favor?" Zeno said, pointing to Shawnm.

"What kind of favor?" Shawnm inquired.

"When we go home, I want to go home with you today," Zeno suggested.

"With me? That's your favor to ask?'" she said. "What's the occasion?"

"Something special," Zeno replied.

"What's that special thing?" she asked.

"You will find out," said Zeno.

"Shouldn't I know before we go?" she asked.

"Yeah, you will know," Zeno assured her. "But not now; later."

"Is that something that just applies to me or all of us?" she inquired.

"It applies to you for today," said Zeno. "But maybe later on. they'll be invited, too."

"Is it a picnic? Or a wedding?" the girl guessed.

"Nothing like that," Zeno replied. "Something far better than that."

"Wow, something far better," she said. "What is it then?"

"I'm afraid you'll take it hard," Zeno explained it, "It's up to you, though. You can say no if you don't feel like it at any time."

"I want to find out what you want to tell me," said Shawnm.

"I'll consider telling you alone," Zeno said.

"Will you guys excuse us for a minute?" Shawnm asked her friends.

" I promise it won't take too long," Zeno said.

They left the room and closed the door behind them.

"Okay," said Shawnm, "tell me what's on your mind?"

"Have you heard the name of that government official, M?" Zeno asked.

"Yeah, I've heard his name, but I don't know the guy," Shawnm replied. "So what about him?"

"He's a friend of my mom," Zeno said.

"Okay, so what's your point?" Shawnm inquired.

"Well, my mom told me one day that I should go to see him," Zeno began. "And before that, my mom told me that he helped us financially." Zeno put her pen between her fingers and played with it. "Anyway, when I went to his home, he told me to wait for him until my mom arrived, and when she got there, he took us to his bedroom, and he start uncovering me right there."

"In front of your mom, you mean?" Shawnm asked.

"Yeah, and he took my virginity," Zeno said.

Shawnm gasped, and her face turned pale and she had a hard time breathing. "So now are you going to get married to him?" Shawnm inquired.

"No, that's not my point," Zeno replied.

"So what's your point?"

"After that, he asked me to bring some of my friends to him, like you," Zeno said frankly.

Shawnm started shaking all over. She found it hard to move her tongue in her mouth while listening to Zeno talk like that, without any respect. She was shocked and her body began trembling.

"I'm sorry; you can say no," Zeno finally said. "Until now, six of my friends came with me, and they all enjoyed it." Zeno try to shake the fear from her, but when Zeno noticed she was shaking, before Zeno could say another word, Shawnm fell to the floor, unconscious. Zeno ran screaming to her friends for help, and they all ran as fast as they could to their friend.

"What happened to her?" they asked.

"I don't know. She suddenly fell to the floor. I didn't do anything to her," Zeno lied.

"That's not true! What did you do to her?" screamed one of them.

"Nothing, I swear," Zeno replied.

"She was fine when we left her," other girl interrupted.

"Did you give her something?" one of the students inquired.

"No, why would I give her a thing?" Zeno replied.

"Let's take her to the office," suggested the girl who screamed.

"She's right," they all agreed.

They grabbed Shawnm by her arms and feet and carried her to the school office, but Zeno was afraid to go with them. The principal, St. Rwpak, was sitting on her seat, working on some documents she has in her hand. She didn't have the slightest idea of what was going on when bunch of students entered the office. Right away, one of the students screamed, "Shawnm is unconscious! You gotta help us!"

"What's going on?" St. Rwpak asked worriedly.

"You don't know what's going on with us?" one of the students inquired, but before the principal could open her mouth, other girl said, "Zeno asked us to go with her to M's house for sex!"

"She is asking you for what?" St. Rwpak shouted, not believing what she heard.

The girl started sobbing. "Every day she sends a truck after us, and the driver asks us to go with him. If we refuse to go, they bother us."

"Who's M?" St. Rwpak inquired. She didn't know what the initial meant, but when the student said his last name, St. Rwpak understood.

"Tell me, why did your friend pass out?" St. Rwpak inquired.

"We don't know. Go ask Zeno," replied same girl.

"Where is Zeno?" St. Rwpak asked.

"She's in the class," they all replied.

"Go get her for me right now," St. Rwpak ordered a student close by. Then the principal helped the girl who passed out to regain her strength. They applied water on her face, and St. Rwpak gave her a glass of cold water to drink. She gulped it down and felt safe in finding herself between St. Rwpak's hands.

"St. Rwpak wants you in the office," the student informed Zeno when she got to the class. Zeno put her phone away and followed her to the office; she was trembling.

"Come forward, Zeno, and tell me the truth. What is going on here?" St. Rwpak demanded.

"I don't take them by force. They follow me of their own will; I swear." Zeno started sobbing.

"Don't cry to cover your guilt," said St. Rwpak angrily. "It doesn't work that way."

"I swear I don't force any of them," Zeno continued to repeat.

"What's that truck's number that follows you—you just mentioned it?" St. Rwpak inquired of the other girls.

"It's 48607 and the color is red," two of the students replied.

St. Rwpak wrote it down on a piece a paper. "Everyone go back to your classes right now," she ordered. "Sit in your places until I send a teacher to your class."

All the students left the office, but St. Rwpak ordered Zeno to stay, along with the girl who passed out earlier. "Tell me," she began, "how many of your friends have you taken to him ?"

"They all come of their will," Zeno sobbed.

"I'm not asking you if they come of their will or not," St. Rwpak corrected her. "Answer me: how many of them? I need the number."

"Until now, just six of them came along," Zeno admitted.

"Just six of them?" St. Rwpak frowned. "It's good we found out now. If not, you might have invited us too, and before we know it, you'd have turned the school into whorehouse."

Zeno remained silent and looked at the floor, while all her body was shaking.

"I'm going to call the police right now and report what was going on in your class," said St. Rwpak. "I'll ask them to come down and investigate the situation with all of you."

St. Rwpak told the officer who answered the phone about the situation, including the time and dates on the calendar. When she hung up, she got the names from Zeno of the girls who Zeno had taken to M's. Then she told the girl who had passed out to go back to class. "Tell the teacher to send all six of those girls to the office right now," St. Rwpak instructed her. "Tell the teacher to bring them here herself."

After a few minutes, the teacher showed up in the principal's office with all six of them.

"Thank you, teacher," said St. Rwpak. "Now you can go back to your class." She turned to the girls. "Close the door, please." One of them closed the door as she was ordered. "Sit down," she order. "This is going to take some time." They all sat down in their chairs, as St. Rwpak began. "Zeno. you were the first one to take all your friends to him, right?"

"Yeah," Zeno replied sheepishly.

"Did you tell him that you would bring your friends to him, or did he ask you to do so?" St. Rwpak inquired.

"He asked me to do so," Zeno replied.

"How did you know the guy?" St. Rwpak inquired.

"He's a friend of Awaz," Zeno reported.

"A friend of Awaz?" St. Rwpak repeated her words.

"Yes, he is," Zeno assured her.

"Where's Awaz? Is she here?" St. Rwpak inquired.

"She's not a student," said Zeno.

"So who she is?" St. Rwpak inquired.

"She's my neighbor," Zeno explained.

"You said she's your mom?" one of the girl said.

"Does your mom know her?" St. Rwpak inquired.

"Yes," Zeno replied.

"She knows that Awaz takes you to this official?" St. Rwpak insisted.

"No, she doesn't," Zeno replied.

The principal gave a big sigh. "Why did you listen to her?" She turned to face the other students. "And why did you follow her when she was misleading you? Why did you listen to Zeno?"

All the students remained silent, not knowing how to respond. After a while, St. Rwpak received a phone call from the police station. She received instructions from the police officer, and upon hanging up the phone, she went to a drawer to take out the file of all of the students and started contacting their families to come to the school right away. "It's an urgent matter," she told each of them. "We'd like to talk to you about your daughter."

When the family members showed up at the principal's office, St. Rwpak explained the situation to them; later, she sent the students home. "I reported the event to the police already. I will discuses the matter with the school board later today, and we will try to find some salvation, so I will inform you of any decision we make." All the girls went back home with their parents, except Zeno. Later on, Zeno's mom showed up in the school office. She didn't know what to say; she was so angry with her neighbor Awaz, she start crying. St. Rwpak consoled her; then she took Zeno and went home.

It was same afternoon when the government official M got a call from Awaz, because St. Rwpak got her number from Zeno and gave it to the police. The government official promised Awaz that he would take care of everything, and he told her not to worry. After few months, he really fulfilled his promise, by punishing St. Rwpak through his power.

The Innocent Principal Transfer

The next morning, all the students, like every other day, went to their classes. No one was suppose to talk about what had happened the day before. St. Rwpak had advised all the students, but the students kept talking about it secretly among themselves, during their break times. They asked their friends who attend the class the day before. That day, St. Rwpak arranged a meeting with all the teachers in the school. After a couple hours of a closed meeting in the school office, they came to that decision to give all of the victims permission this year to stay in their homes and come back the next year to finish school, so their futures would not be at risk for the rest of their lives. St. Rwpak contacted their families and told them about the decision. At first, the families were okay with it, but one day, after four weeks, the principal received a phone call from someone who claimed to be one of the victims' fathers, He told the principal that he would not let her stay in her job and that she would be fired before the year ended. St. Rwpak thought it was a father who was disappointed about his daughter's future.

All final examinations ended on time, and school closed for summer. The second round of examinations started in August, and during this time St. Rwpak got a phone call from the chief officer of the board of education, telling her that she had been transferred to a different school as a teacher. But she wasn't in the school that day; her assistant, St. Shler, took the call, so he left a message for St. Rwpak with St. Shler. That day, St. Rwpak went on a picnic with her husband, who was an electric engineer and worked in the electric power office as a part-time job in the afternoon. During the day, St. Rwpak's husband worked at his shop, the Electric Ray at Night. He usually went home after ten o'clock every night.

It was Saturday night before St. Rwpak thought about school. She got her cell phone and called St. Shler's number to see how things had gone on at school. They first discussed the students' performance that year. St. Rwpak said, "We have only one month left of summer vacation. School will open next month, as you know. I hope our school this year will stay at top of other schools, like pervious years."

"I hope so, too," answered St. Shler, "but I'm afraid this year our school is a little bit lower, especially after what happened last spring."

"I'm also a little bit concerned about that, too," St. Rwpak agreed. "Because it's affected all of us, not only our students. It shocked us all."

"Still, I believe our students work on their assignments, according to what I saw in their grades. Last week I checked last year's documents and I'm grateful for the results."

"So, how was school last Thursday? The examination of the second round went well?" St. Rwpak inquired.

"It was fine, and everything went smoothly, " St. Shler replied. "By the way, someone from the board of education office called. The man said he wanted to talk to you about your transfer, so I told him that you were on vacation."

"My transfer?" St. Rwpak inquired. "That's strange."

"Something else happened later," St. Shler continued.

"What was it?"

"Around two o'clock in the afternoon, just before I went home, someone showed up in the office. He said he came from the board of education office and he had a file in his hands. He asked for you, but when I told him that you were on vacation, he took out a closed envelope from the file."

"For me?" St. Rwpak asked.

"I—"

The phone connection was cut suddenly. St. Rwpak tried to reconnect, but when she dialed the number, it didn't ring. Instead, she got an automated message from the phone company, telling her, "The number you've called is closed or out of service."

She kept trying to reconnect, and finally, after fifteen minutes, the call went through. "Sorry about the disconnect. The line's evil," St. Rwpak apologized.

"Don't worry," St. Shler replied.

"So what happened after that?" St. Rwpak inquired.

"Nothing special. I just got the letter and kept it in the drawer of your desk," St. Shler explained.

"You didn't open it?" St. Rwpak asked.

"No, I didn't?" replied St. Shler.

"I wish you had," said St. Rwpak. "But I'll find out tomorrow when I come to school."

St. Rwpak hung up the phone, and started reading a book while the electric was on. Before too long, the power went off, so she closed the book in her hand and lit the oil lamp. Covering herself with a blanket, she fell asleep.

When she rose from her bed, it was 6:40 AM. Her husband and kids were still sleeping, but she went to the kitchen and filled the kettle with water. She placed it on the stove, lit the gas, and then went to the bathroom. When she came out, she called to her husband to wake up, just as his clock's alarm start ringing. Her husband grabbed the clock and pushed the button to stop it. After they finished their breakfast, she changed her clothes and rode the bus to school. Her husband stayed with the kids until later, when he would take them to his father's home before going to work.

When St. Rwpak got in school, she asked St. Shler about the man who'd brought the letter. "Will he call back today?" St. Rwpak wondered. "I didn't ask to get transferred as I told you, but I don't know if any other teacher asked for it. Still, that teacher should let me know if that's the case."

St. Rwpak puzzled about her transfer, she don't want to leave her school after so many years serving in that school, but if the bord of education want to, she has no choice either take it, or leave the school at once, that she don't want to leave her profession

"Maybe, but I'm sure the man mentioned your name," said St. Shler.

"Even if they want to transfer me, they should send the official letter and explain the reason, not just in a phone call," said St. Rwpak.

"I agree that's what they're suppose to do" said St. Shler, "but maybe that's what the letter is about."

"You said it's in the drawer?" inquired St. Rwpak.

"Yes, it is."

"Thanks" said St. Rwpak

St. Rwpak went into her office, along with St. Shler, and took the letter from the drawer. It had a return address of the board of education office. She opened the letter and then sat in her swivel chair to read it. St. Shler gazed at her, waiting for her to finish. Finally, she started reading aloud to St. Shler:

From: the chief officer of the board of education
To: St. Rwpak, principal of Sunshine High School for Girls
> After the final decision at our board members meeting, which took place last week, we decided to transfer you from your existing school, Sunshine High School for Girls, as a principal to the Shade of Hope High

School for Girls as a biology teacher, which was your profession for ten years of service, before you became a principal. One month from receiving this notice, you should start your new position.

Note: Further information is not available at his time. There is a chance that we're in need of a biology teacher right now, so most of the schools don't have a biology teacher at the moment. We know that your school has other teachers who can teach biology. We will notify you by mail or you will receive guidance from the office of Shade of Hope High School. Please contact your new school office administration about your transfer in the future.

Sincerely,
The General Principal for the Board of Education
May 20, 2005

"That's how they reward someone for serving with the best attitude and being polite in all the situations, to serving the country and people, and for bringing the new generations to the straight path, and working toward success for a better educational level in the country?" said St. Rwpak, a former principal, now the innocent teacher with a melancholy voice. She grabbed her purse, took her cell phone out, and dialed the number of her husband. He didn't answer the phone, so she put the phone back in her purse and start hugging St. Shler. They cried for fifteen minutes and finally let each other go. St. Rwpak took her belongings and went out from the office. She never came back.

The End